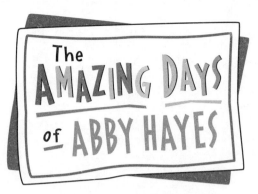

The AMAZING DAYS of ABBY HAYES

Volume Three

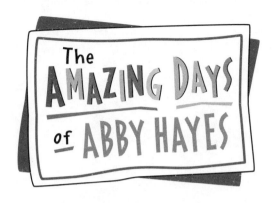

Volume Three

ANNE MAZER

SCHOLASTIC INC.
New York Toronto London Auckland Sydney
Mexico City New Delhi Hong Kong Buenos Aires

Two Heads Are Better Than One, ISBN 0-439-35366-1, Copyright © 2002 by Anne Mazer.

The More, the Merrier, ISBN 0-439-35367-X, Copyright © 2002 by Anne Mazer.

Out of Sight, Out of Mind, ISBN 0-439-35368-8, Copyright © 2002 by Anne Mazer. Interior illustrations by Monica Gesue.

12 11 10 9 8 7 6 5 4 3 2 1   6 7 8 9 10/0

Printed in the U.S.A.   23

This edition created exclusively for Barnes & Noble, Inc.

2006 Barnes & Noble Books

ISBN 0-7607-9602-5

First compilation printing, January 2006

Contents

The AMAZING DAYS of ABBY HAYES

Two Heads Are Better Than One

To all the students in the Cortland city school district:
Randall, Smith, Virgil, Barry, and Parker Elementary Schools.
With a special thank-you for an unforgettable birthday
to the students at Virgil and Randall!

Chapter 1

Thursday morning

"When the head aches, all members share the pain."

—Cervantes

Brace and Bandage Calendar

Does that mean family members? I wish they'd share my pain. There is plenty to go around. My head aches, my arms ache, my legs ache — even my eyelashes ache!

I have been home with the flu for four days now. It feels like forever!

Advantages of Being Sick:
1. Can watch as much TV as I want.
2. No school or homework.
3. No chores.
4. Sleep all day.
5. Meals in room.

<u>Disadvantages of Being Sick:</u>
1. Too tired to watch TV.
2. Behind on schoolwork.
3. Bored. Achy. Feverish.
4. Crumbs in bed.
5. I miss my friends!

Last week, seven people in our class were out with the flu.

Brianna and Bethany came down with it on the same day. (Bethany <u>always</u> imitates Brianna!)

Mason turned green in the middle of the math quiz. (How did he time that just right?)

Jessica was out for ten days. (My best friend has asthma, which makes every cold or flu worse.)

Natalie was absent for only two days. (My other best friend hardly ever gets sick.)

Zach was so ill he didn't want to play computer games. (Can this be true?)

Ms. Bunder got the flu and had to cancel creative writing class! (Boo-hoo! Ms.

Bunder, why did you get sick last week instead of this week?)

This morning I got out of bed for the
first time in days. I went downstairs.
Everyone was eating breakfast.
"You look like a ghost," said my older
sister Eva. She is too healthy to get the
flu. She drinks power shakes and exercises
every two minutes.
"Take vitamins," said Eva's twin, Isabel.
If Isabel got the flu, she would put it
under a microscope and study it. Or write
a paper about it. She wouldn't lie in bed
and moan.
My little brother, Alex, looked scared
when he saw me. "Will Abby have to go
to the hospital?" he asked.
I tried to say, "I'm okay," but I
croaked like a frog instead.

Help! I am turning into a ghost-frog! No
one in my family has the flu except me.
They are all at school or work. Dad is

upstairs in his home office. He gave me a bell to ring if I need him. I have a glass of water by the bed and a box of tissues. The TV is in my room but I think I'll go to sleep again...

Abby turned over in bed and looked at the clock. It was three-thirty in the afternoon. She had slept through most of the day again.

Slowly she moved her arms and legs. She felt less achy but she was still congested. When was she going to get better?

The telephone rang. A minute later, a gentle knock sounded at the door.

"Abby? Are you up?" It was Alex.

"Come in, Alex." Abby blew her nose loudly.

"Jessica's on the phone." He handed her the cordless telephone.

"Hi, Jessica," Abby said hoarsely to her best friend.

"How are you?" Jessica said. "We miss you in school!"

Abby lay back on the pillow. "This morning I wrote in my journal for fifteen minutes. Then I slept for the rest of the day!" She coughed. "I miss everyone, too."

"You sound terrible," Jessica said.

"I *am* terrible," Abby agreed. "So terrible that no one will get near me. You should have seen Alex run out of my room just now."

"He doesn't want to get sick," Jessica said. She was always practical.

"It's not fair!" Abby wailed. "Why am I the only one in my family with the flu?"

"Everyone's had it in school," Jessica said consolingly. "Ms. Kantor was out on Monday and Tuesday. She sounds as bad as you."

Ms. Kantor was their fifth-grade classroom teacher.

"We're starting a new unit in science about astronomy," Jessica announced. She sounded excited. Astronomy was one of her favorite subjects.

Abby blew her nose again. At least they weren't studying germs. "What else are we doing?"

"In creative writing, Ms. Bunder had us write sonnets. We had a multiplication quiz and read a chapter of *Tuck Everlasting*. Ms. Kantor handed out astronomy fact sheets."

"I got a C– on my electromagnetic report," Abby groaned, "and now I'm missing astronomy. Not to mention multiplication quizzes and sonnets."

"Don't worry, you'll catch up," Jessica reassured her.

Abby closed her eyes. "Great," she muttered. "I can't wait."

"I asked Ms. Kantor for your assignments," Jessica said. "So you won't get too far behind. My mom and I will drop them off a little later."

"Thanks," Abby said. "I hope I can do them."

"Oh! I almost forgot!" Jessica cried. "Ms. Kantor announced that the fifth grade is having a science fair this year."

"Science fair?"

"We're doing it with Mrs. McMillan's class. The teachers are assigning partners tomorrow. And Ms. Kantor said we'll have a chance to get extra credit."

Abby suddenly felt exhausted. Too much was happening. She didn't want to think about science fairs and extra credit and partners with another class. She didn't want to think about astronomy units and bad grades and sonnets and homework assignments. She just wanted to sleep.

"I have to go," she croaked. "I can't talk any-more."

"Get better soon!" Jessica said.

When she woke up, it was dark and the smell of dinner filled the house. For the first time in days, Abby was hungry. She slowly got out of bed and put on her old blue bathrobe. She ran a brush through her tangled, snarly hair and tried to smile at her pale reflection in the mirror.

She *did* look like a ghost! A hideous, disheveled ghost! And a hungry one.

"You're out of bed! Are you feeling better?" her mother asked. Olivia Hayes wore the gray pin-striped suit that she put on for court appearances. Her hair was done up in a bun and she wore a gold and pearl necklace.

"I just got home," she said. "Your father told me you slept all day."

"Uh-huh," Abby said. Her throat didn't feel as sore and her limbs didn't ache as much as they had.

Her mother put her hand on Abby's forehead. "Your fever is gone. Are you coming down for dinner? Your father made roast chicken and potatoes."

"Yes," Abby said. "I'm starved."

"That's great!" Her mother smiled at her. "You're starting to get better."

Abby leaned against her mother. "I'm sick of being sick!"

"'This, too, will pass,'" her mother said, giving Abby a hug.

"*When* will it pass?" Abby asked. "I want to go back to school!"

Her mother shook her head. "Probably not until Monday."

"Awwwww," Abby said.

Her mother smiled. "I don't hear that very often." She hugged Abby again. "I'm going to make the salad for dinner. Why don't you wash up and come downstairs?"

Abby headed for the bathroom. Her walk was slow and shuffling. She felt like a patient in a hospital ward. In front of the mirror, she stared at her pale face, limp hair, and blinking eyes.

"You look awful," she told herself.

She washed her hands and splashed water on her chin and cheeks.

"What is wrong with this face?" she asked. "Find three problems and win a prize."

She squirted scented body lotion onto her arms and neck and face.

"Problem one, hollow cheeks," Abby said. "Problem two, circles under eyes. Problem three, cracked, dry lips. Where's my prize?"

She found Eva's raspberry kiwi lip gloss in a drawer. Pretending it was lipstick, Abby coated her lips. She pinched her cheeks to redden them.

She pulled on a strand of her hair. It was usually curly and wild and red. Today it was lifeless and dull and pale. Had the flu even drained the energy from her hair?

A pair of scissors lay on the shelf. She picked them up and snipped at the ends of a curl. It bounced back around her face.

"That's better," she said.

She clipped at it some more. Just an inch or two shorter was all she needed. And maybe she could cut the worst snarls instead of combing them out.

She wetted down her hair and shaped the sides, the front, and the top. She cut out a few snarls. Then she fluffed her hair with her fingertips and trimmed some more.

Abby smiled. She had never known she could cut

her own hair. It was easy. Why didn't she do this all the time?

"Dinner!" Alex yelled.

"Coming!" Abby cried hoarsely. "Just a minute."

She aimed the blow-dryer at her hair, scrunching the curls in her hand. In a minute, her hair was dry.

Abby stood back to survey the results in the bathroom mirror.

Her hair looked like someone had cut it with a jigsaw. It was uneven and raggedy. She hadn't trimmed and shaped, she had hacked and slashed.

It was the most awful haircut she had ever seen.

Chapter 2

Thursday | evening

"No man can lose what he
never had."

—Izaak Walton

Disappearing Acts Calendar

Not true! I lost my hair AND my hair-cut. They're in the bathroom garbage pail nestled in with used Band-Aids, Q-Tips, and disposable razors.

<u>What I had (and lost)</u>:
A hairdo.

<u>What I have (and wish I could lose)</u>:
A scare-do.

Can't tape, glue, or paste my hair back together again! (I tried.)

(Now understand how Humpty-Dumpty felt.)

News Flash! Horrible Hair Hidden Under Hot Hat!

As Alex Hayes called her to dinner, Abby Hayes stared with dismay at her reflection in the mirror. Her hands strayed to her shorn locks. She tried in vain to force them into shape.

What would her family say when they saw her horrible haircut? They would make jokes, ask unpleasant questions, tease her, and shake their heads.

"Dinner!" Alex yelled again. "We're waiting for you!"

Abby plopped a towel on her head, then  a shower cap. Neither worked. She dashed into her bedroom, found a striped wool hat, and shoved it on her head.

A few straggling curls stuck out. She

tucked them into the hat. Then she went downstairs.

The entire Hayes family was sitting at the table when she came downstairs. Everyone looked at Abby as she took her place between Alex and Isabel.

The tragic ten-year-old held her breath. She was sure her mother or father would ask her to take off the hat at the table. Someone was bound to ask why she was wearing a wool hat to dinner in 75-degree weather.

Paul Hayes smiled. "Good to see you among the living again, Abby."

"Yeah," Abby mumbled. She pulled the hat down over her ears.

"Are you feeling chilled?" Olivia Hayes asked with a concerned frown. "Is your fever up again? You look flushed."

Eva jumped to her feet. "I'll get an afghan!"

"I'm okay," Abby said. She helped herself to a large piece of chicken and a baked potato.

"You're sure?" her mother said again.

"My head is a little cold, that's all," Abby muttered.

The Hayes family expressed concern and worry. Olivia Hayes said Abby could eat upstairs in her room. Isabel offered to serve her dinner in bed. Alex said he would read her a story.

Abby Hayes politely declined all offers of help. She pretended to be brave. She didn't pretend to be hungry. She ate two pieces of chicken and a whole baked potato with butter. She also drank a huge glass of milk.

When Abby went back to her room, she took the hat off. She was flushed and sweaty from wearing a wool hat on a warm evening. Her hair looked even worse than she remembered!

What will Abby Hayes do?

Stay tuned for further reports!

This is Abby again. (I wish it wasn't.)

I wish I was Natalie with short hair. I wish I was Jessica with long, straight hair. I even wish I was Brianna with perfect hair!

I wish I was anyone but me!

What I Look Like:
A lawn mower ran over my head.
I cut my hair blindfolded.
The revenge of the scissors!

Solutions (I hope):
1. Glue hat to head. (Too hot. Hair won't grow right.)
2. Shave head. (Will look like newborn baby or male wrestler.)
3. Buy wig. (It's not Halloween.)
4. Don't come out of room until hair grows back. (Will miss spring and summer.)

I want my hair back! Now!!!

Later Thursday evening:

Jessica dropped off my homework. Alex brought it upstairs. I was reading Tuck Everlasting. It was pretty good. It was helping me forget my problems when Mom knocked on the door.

The Unkindest Cut: A Play with One Part (down the middle of my head)

by Abby Hayes

Act I

Mom: Abby? Can I come in?

Abby is a ten-year-old girl recovering from the flu. She is wearing purple pajamas. Her curly red hair has a ragged appearance. At the sound of her mother's voice, Abby grabs a wool hat with lightning speed.

Abby: Just a minute!

Mom is a lawyer and a mother of four. She is carrying a shower cap and a pair of scissors. A few stray red curls dangle from her hand. As she enters the room, she looks suspiciously at the wool hat on her daughter's head.

Mom: Hi, Abby.

Abby tries to say something but her stomach is sinking.

She speaks directly to audience: Why do stomachs sink? They aren't ships or boats.

She quickly recovers: Hi, Mom.

Mom: How are you feeling?

Abby (tries to look innocent): Congested, Mom. What's up?

Mom (directs a searching look at her daughter. Her eyes are like lighthouse beams or high-powered flashlights): I found these scissors and shower cap and this hair in the bathroom.

Abby: Really?

Mom: Mmm-hmmm.

Abby (puts on astonished expression): That's amazing.

Mom: Is that all you have to say?

Abby (nods): Yes.

Mom (points to the wool cap on her daughter's head): What's underneath that hat, Abby?

Abby (stomach sinking to the bottom of the ocean): Not much, Mom.

Mom: Take it off.

Abby slowly and reluctantly pulls the cap from her head.

Mom (stares): I can't believe this.

Abby says nothing.

Mom: Why did you try to cut it your-self? What were you thinking?

Abby: I looked awful!

Mom shakes her head. She sighs loudly.

Abby (despairingly): Now I look worse!

Mom: Maybe it's not as bad as it looks.

Abby: It is.

Mom: Let me see what I can do. (She picks up hairbrush and begins brushing daughter's hair.)

Abby: Don't bother.

Mom (stands back to check the results): You're right. It _is_ as bad as it looks.

Abby: I _told_ you.

Mom (glances at scissors): Maybe I can trim it a little.

Abby (suddenly hopeful): Can you even it out?

Mom: Of course I can. I have an ob-jective eye.

Abby (again speaks directly to the audi-ence): What is an objective eye? A legal term that Mom uses in court? Or some kind of grammar?

Snippets of hair fall to the floor as her mother trims and clips.

Abby: All I want is a hairdo instead of a scare-do.

Mom: Next time, ask me for help. A shampoo and a hot bath would have made all the difference. It's normal to look awful after a week in bed.

Abby (nods): Okay, Mom. I'll remember that. Thanks for helping now.

Mom (hands her daughter the mirror): You're welcome.

As the act ends, Abby looks eagerly into the mirror.

Act II

The curtain rises. Abby Hayes, age ten, stares in horror at her face in the mirror.

Mom (apologetically): Sorry. I didn't improve it, did I?

Abby: Not much.

Abby (to the audience): My mother knows all about briefs, torts, and affidavits. She knows about running long distances, running a household, and serving on community boards. But she doesn't know anything about cutting hair!

(Despairingly) <u>Why</u> don't they teach that in law school?

Mom: Your sister Isabel did a good job of cutting my hair once.

Abby: NO!

Mom: Maybe she can give us some advice.

Mom exits room. Comes back with Isabel.

Isabel (picks up scissors): I know what to do.

Abby: <u>Don't!</u>

Isabel (puts down scissors): I don't want to cut it, anyway. It's hard to cut curly hair. Mom's is nice and straight. Yours is unpredictable.

Abby (sarcastic): Thanks, sis.

Enter Eva: Need some help?

Mom and Isabel: We're trying to figure out what to do with Abby's hair.

Eva (studies her younger sister): Forget it. It's hopeless.

Abby (very sarcastic): Thanks a <u>lot</u>.

<u>Final Act</u>

The curtain rises. Abby looks at herself

in the mirror. There is an expression of terror and deep despair on her face.

Her mother and sisters surround her. They sing their regrets in a chorus.

The curtain falls.

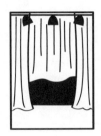

Backstage After the Play:

My hair looked like a battlefield. It looked like a football field after a scrimmage. It looked like a courtroom riot.

"Too many chefs spoil the 'do,'" my mother said sadly. "I made it worse."

"I thought that was impossible," I said.

My father came into the room. For a moment, he was speechless. "Is there a professional on the premises?" he finally asked.

"I'll make her an appointment first thing tomorrow morning," my mother said. She looked embarrassed.

"Hair today, gone tomorrow," my father joked.

I scowled at him. "That's so funny I forgot to laugh."

"By tomorrow, this will all be a memory," my mother promised. "Jeannie's the best in town. She'll give you a haircut that'll make you forget this one. I'll get you to her right after school."

I coughed and blew my nose to remind everyone how sick I was. "For your information, I am _not_ going to school tomorrow!"

(Even if I wanted to go to school, I'd _never_ show up with this haircut. I'd faint first. I'd run a fever. I'd develop a terrible lingering disease. I'd...)

Fortunately, I don't have to. I'm still weak from the flu. I will spend Friday drinking orange juice and trying to catch up on my homework. Dad will take me to get my hair cut later in the day.

Chapter 3

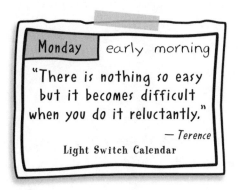

Monday | early morning

"There is nothing so easy
but it becomes difficult
when you do it reluctantly."
— Terence
Light Switch Calendar

What should be easy:
Getting up.
Brushing hair.
Walking to school.

All of these things are difficult because
I don't want to do them!

Why they are difficult:
I have to look at my hair in the mirror.
I have to walk outside with my hair.
I have to go to school with my hair.

<u>Why they are especially difficult:</u>

The haircutter is out of town until Thursday afternoon! She's the only one I trust to cut my hair.

I wonder if Ms. Kantor will let me wear a hat in class. (Probably not.)

Can I tape leaves onto my head and pretend I'm a tree? (Idea for science fair project.)

Or put a paper bag over my head and say I'm a walking sculpture? (Get extra credit in art.)

Abby walked onto the school playground with her best friends, Natalie and Jessica.

"There ought to be a haircut hospital," she said. "With ambulance service. Call 911 for hair emergencies."

"You'll be okay," Jessica said reassuringly. She was a tall girl with long, straight brown hair that she wore in a ponytail. "No one will notice."

"Oh, yeah?" Abby said.

Natalie adjusted the strap of her backpack. She

was a slight girl with short, dark hair who never paid much attention to her appearance. "Tell everyone you did it on purpose. Or that it was a side effect of the flu. Laugh it off."

"I should have shaved it off!" Abby cried. "And gone to school bald. Wait until Brianna sees it!"

Brianna was one of their classmates. She had perfect hair, dressed like a model, took French and acting lessons, and was always the best at everything.

"Don't worry about her," Jessica said.

"Today we meet with our partners for the science fair," Natalie said.

"I can't wait!" Jessica cried. "This is going to be so much fun!"

"Who did you get for partners?" Abby asked. She tugged on the cotton hat that Jessica had lent her. Before they had left for school, her friends had put barrettes and clips in her hair. It had improved the look a little.

"Sarah is my partner," Jessica said. "She's interested in ecology and the environment. We're going to study the effect of pollution on viewing stars at night."

"I got paired with Dylan and Amanda," Natalie said. "We went to the park this weekend and decided to grow crystals for our project."

"What should *I* do?" Abby asked her friends. "Study the structure of a hair molecule? Analyze the difference between curly and straight hair? Find out how fast hair grows after it's cut?"

"Get your mind off your hair, Abby," Jessica advised.

"My hair is on my mind," Abby said. "Get it?"

Her friends stared at her.

"That's the kind of bad joke my father loves," Abby explained.

The three girls walked up the stairs to the school. Their classmates greeted them.

"Spelling test today!" Mason yelled at them.

Abby shrugged. She had studied all the words over the weekend. Besides, spelling was easy. It was a lot easier than math. It was easier than science, too. She wouldn't need any extra credit in spelling.

Ahead of them, Brianna and Bethany were talking about their weekend. As usual, Brianna was the best-dressed girl in the fifth grade. She was wearing a short mirrored dress and chunky shoes. Her glossy dark hair was perfectly cut.

Bethany looked like the mirror image of her best friend. She was also wearing a short dress and chunky shoes. Her hair was blonde and braided with ribbons. She looked like Brianna, but she was a lot nicer — especially on her own.

"My hamster Blondie had babies this weekend," Bethany announced to the fifth graders around her. "Does anyone want one?"

Brianna frowned in irritation. "Is that all you think about?" she asked Bethany. "Hamsters?"

Bethany looked hurt. "They're so cute."

"Let's talk about *me* for a change," Brianna said. "This weekend I won a sailing race on the lake."

"I'd like a hamster," Natalie interrupted. "If my parents will let me have one."

"Ask them as soon as you can," Bethany said. "If I can't give them away, my mother said I'd have to bring them to the pet store."

"I came in way ahead of everyone else," Brianna continued. "Bethany! Are you listening?"

"Sure," Bethany said. "Yay, Brianna. You're the best."

Jessica rolled her eyes. "There they go again."

The three friends walked into their classroom together.

"Abby! You're back!" Ms. Kantor exclaimed. "It's good to have you in the classroom again. I hope you're feeling better."

Abby handed her teacher a written excuse and the makeup homework she had done over the weekend. "I'm better," she said.

"At least until I take my hat off," she added under her breath. Her heart began to thump. Ms. Kantor had a "no hats" rule. Any minute now, she'd ask Abby to take it off. Or maybe she wouldn't notice?

Abby sat down at her desk and took pencil and paper out of her backpack. Her classmates took their places around her.

The bell rang. Morning announcements began.

"Good morning," the principal, Ms. Yang, said over the loudspeaker. "All rise for the Pledge."

Abby stood up and put her right hand over her heart. "I pledge allegiance . . ." she recited.

"You forgot to take off your hat," Ms. Kantor whispered to her.

". . . to the flag . . ." Slowly Abby reached up to remove the cotton hat. She glanced around the room to see if anyone was watching.

". . . of the United States of America . . ."

Abby dropped the hat onto her desk and automatically repeated the words of the Pledge. Her face was hot — and no one had said a word! How was she going to stand it when everyone teased her?

". . . with liberty and justice for all," she finished. Liberty — that's what she would have once she got a proper haircut. She hoped Jeannie would do justice to her hair.

The class sat down.

Over the loudspeaker, a third grader started reading a poem about pigs.

Brianna nudged her. "What happened?" she whispered, pointing to Abby's head.

Abby groaned. "Family haircut," she whispered back.

"They're the worst," Brianna said. "Hair torture."

"Yes!" Abby agreed.

"I know about bad hair days," Brianna confessed.

"*You* do?"

"You can borrow my hair gel at recess," she offered. "It's the best."

"Wow. Th-th-thanks," Abby stammered. She had never expected Brianna to be sympathetic.

The announcements ended.

"We're going to get together with our science project partners in the library," Ms. Kantor announced. "I hope you all came up with ideas for projects this weekend."

A dozen hands shot into the air.

Ms. Kantor smiled. "We'll discuss them in a few minutes," she said. "If you don't have a partner yet, we'll give you one. Mrs. McMillan and I hope this will be the first of many projects our classes will work on together."

As Abby walked to the library, her classmates chattered excitedly about their projects. No one commented about her hair.

Abby hurried down the hallway to catch up with her friends.

"I'm going to grow molds," Mason announced loudly. He burped. "Kyle and I are going to have the most disgusting science project in the school."

"That's easy," Jessica said under her breath. "They're the two most disgusting boys in the school."

"I'm going to write a computer program," Zach said. "Tyler and I got paired with Daniel. He knows as much about computers as we do."

Abby was silent. She hadn't given any thought to her project because she didn't know who her partner might be. Abby hoped it was a girl who liked the same things she did. Someone who loved writing and Rollerblading and the color purple.

In the library, the students drifted into groups of two and three. Abby went up to Ms. Kantor.

"I know, Abby, you don't have a partner," Ms. Kantor said with a smile.

She looked down at a list of names. "Mrs. McMillan and I are hoping that you will learn new things about science and make a new friend, too."

"Sure, Ms. Kantor. My mother says you can never have enough friends."

"Let's see. Your partner will be Casey Hoffman, who just transferred from another school."

"Okay." Abby didn't know Casey Hoffman, but she'd be glad to show her the ropes.

"This project will be a part of your grade," Ms. Kantor explained. "You can earn extra credit for a difficult or elaborate project."

"Jessica told me."

Ms. Kantor gestured to Mrs. McMillan. "Send Casey over." She picked up her folder. "You two will get along well," she predicted.

Abby waited in front of a rack of paperback books. How did Ms. Kantor know that she would get along well with Casey? What if Casey was like Brianna? Or if she didn't like anything that Abby did? Or if —

"Did someone cut your hair with a lawn mower?" It was a boy Abby didn't know. He had dark eyes, dark hair, and ears that stuck out.

Abby had written the same thing in her journal just a day ago. It was one thing, however, to write it herself in the privacy of her room and another to hear a boy say it loudly in the middle of a crowded school library.

"No, they cut it with a nail scissors!" Abby retorted.

"In the dark?" he asked with a huge grin on his face.

"How'd you guess?" Abby asked.

He folded his arms across his chest. "High IQ."

"Does that stand for Idiotic Quotes?" Abby shot back at him. "Or Ignorant Questions?"

"Impossible Quizzes," the boy said.

"Ha, ha," Abby said. She glanced around the room. There was no sign of her partner.

"Don't you have a science fair project to work on?" she asked.

"Don't you?" he mimicked.

"I'm waiting for my partner," Abby said. "She'll be here any minute. You better go find yours."

"I know who my partner is," the boy said.

"Oh, yeah?" Abby said. "Why don't you go find him?" *Get lost,* she added silently. *Go bother some-one else.*

"*Her,*" he corrected. "My partner is a girl." The grin on his face widened.

"So???"

Ms. Kantor hurried toward them. "Have you two begun work on your project yet? Do you need help?"

"Everything's great," the boy said.

"No, it's not!" Abby retorted.

"We've got plenty of ideas," the boy said.

"No, we don't," Abby said. "Ms. Kantor, I need to find my partn — "

She suddenly stopped. Why hadn't she put two and two together? Why hadn't she seen what — or who — was right in front of her nose?

"Good." Ms. Kantor consulted her list. "I won't worry about you. I know you'll both do just fine."

Abby turned to face the boy.

"You're — " The words dried up in her mouth.

The boy nodded. "I'm Casey Hoffman. I'm your science fair partner."

Chapter 4

Wednesday

"Two heads are better than one."

Troll and Monster Calendar

It depends which two!

<u>Head One:</u>

Abby Hayes. A bad haircut and a good mind. At least, it's a good mind for some things. I have good ideas for science fair projects (after consulting a lot of books in the library).

Examples:

1. How does water move through a leaf?

2. Do cats' eyes glow in the dark?

3. What causes dew?

Head Two:

Casey Hoffman. An ordinary haircut and an evil mind. Proof of evilness: constant jokes about my hair.

Example:

"You must be hair-brained!" Laughs. "Ha, ha, ha. Get it?"

Other proof of evilness: his science fair project ideas.

Examples (there are millions):

1. He wants to study different parts of the fingernail and toenail. (Exciting.)

2. He wants to test our reflexes. He throws cotton balls at my face, and everyone in the class watches me blink. (Forget it!)

3. He wants to breed fruit flies and maggots on decomposing bananas. (Ugh! Ugh! UGH!)

Final ultimate proof of evilness:

He calls me "Hayes." And pretends to sneeze when he

Achoo!

sees me. "I have Hayes fever," he says. "Ha, ha, ha. Get it?"

These two heads are not better than one. They cancel each other out. We spent the entire hour arguing. We have not decided on a science fair project.

If I don't do the science fair project, I'm going to get a really bad grade in science. If I do a last-minute science fair project, I won't get the extra credit that I need.

And it's all Casey's fault.

I hate him! I hate him! I <u>hate</u> him!

"Your hair doesn't look too bad today," Jessica commented. She twirled around on the swing. "Is it growing out already?"

"Brianna lent me her hair gel," Abby said. "That stuff really works. It glued down the sticking-out parts."

"*Brianna* lent you her hair gel?" Natalie repeated. "Are you serious?"

It was recess. The spring sun was hot. The three friends were on the swings, talking.

"She said it was the best," Abby said. She leaned back and looked up at the sky. "And she was right."

"You get it cut tomorrow," Jessica reminded her, twirling in the other direction.

"Jeannie better do a good job!" Abby sat up again. "I'm sick of barrettes, bows, and Brianna's gel. I like to brush my hair once in the morning and forget about it."

"How's your science fair project coming?" Natalie asked Abby.

"Ugh!" Abby groaned. "Casey is a case."

"Dylan is nice," Natalie said. "So is Amanda. She invited me to go swimming with her this weekend."

Jessica took a package of gum from her pocket. She unwrapped a piece and put it in her mouth. "Sarah and I are going to the library Friday after school."

"Does everyone like their partner except me?" Abby cried.

Natalie pointed to Bethany, who stood at the edge of the playground. She was watching her best friend Brianna. Brianna was laughing with Victoria, her partner from the other class.

"Bethany doesn't like *Brianna's* partner," Natalie said.

"That's different," Abby said. She began to pump

her legs. The swing rose into the air. "She doesn't have to work with her."

"Bethany looks really unhappy," Natalie said. "I feel sorry for her."

"That's what she gets for being friends with Brianna," Jessica said.

Brianna and Victoria shrieked, then grabbed each other's hands. A look of misery passed over Bethany's face.

Natalie waved at her. "Bethany! Come here!" she yelled. "I want to talk about Blondie's baby hamsters!"

"If that doesn't cheer Bethany up, nothing will," Abby said, skidding to a stop.

Bethany approached the three friends.

"Hi," she said. She sat down between Abby and Jessica.

"My parents said I can have a hamster," Natalie told her. "I just have to keep its cage clean and make sure it doesn't escape."

"Blondie was up all night on her wheel," Bethany said. "She kept waking me up. Are you sure you want a hamster?"

"Yes!" Natalie said.

"I'm constructing a maze for Blondie for the science fair," Bethany confided. Her eyes followed

Brianna and Victoria across the playground.

"Who's your partner?" Abby asked.

"Crystal," Bethany said.

"That name reminds me of a chandelier," Abby said. "Or something that breaks."

"Crystal is the kind of person who breaks things," Bethany said gloomily. "She's nice, but she's not much help."

Jessica jumped up. "There's Sarah!" She waved at a short, plump girl with curly brown hair who was kicking a soccer ball.

Sarah kicked the soccer ball in Jessica's direction. Jessica rushed to intercept it. The two girls passed the ball back and forth.

"They're good, aren't they?" Natalie said. She didn't like sports, although her parents kept trying to make her participate.

Abby felt a twinge of jealousy. She liked soccer, but she wasn't that good. And she wasn't interested in ecology or astronomy.

It was bad enough that she didn't like her science fair partner. It was even worse that her best friend liked hers so much.

"Aaaachooo! Aaaachooo!" The sound of loud, fake sneezing came from behind them.

The three girls turned around.

"Aaaa*chhoooo*!" Casey said.

"We don't want your germs," Abby said. "Go away."

"Awwwwww," Casey said.

"That means get *lost*," Abby said. "Understand?"

He grinned. "I thought you'd be nicer, Hayes."

"Hayes?" Natalie looked at Abby. "Is that what he calls you?"

Abby tried to shrug it off. She blushed furiously instead. Great. Now she was as red as her hair.

"I have an idea for our science project, Hayes." Casey stuck his hands in his pockets. "You're gonna like this one."

Abby glared at him. "If it involves throwing objects at my face or growing slimy molds, I won't do it."

"Picky, picky," Casey said. "How about extracting salt from seawater?"

"Boring."

Natalie nudged her. "That could be fun."

"No," Abby said.

"We could make a study of animal tracks."

Bethany nodded her head in agreement, but Abby ignored her.

"No," she said again.

"Why not?" Casey demanded.

"Because," Abby said.

There was a short silence.

"Do you have a better idea?" Casey said.

"We could experiment with natural dyes," Abby said after a moment. "My neighbor, Heather, uses onionskins and dried flowers to dye yarn."

"I'm not doing anything with yarn!" Casey said. "Knitting is for girls."

"Men used to knit for a living hundreds of years ago," Abby informed him. "Heather told me all about it."

"They don't do it today, Hayes."

"Stop calling me Hayes," Abby said. She looked to her friends for support. "We're never going to agree!"

Natalie jumped up. "I have an idea. I'll be the judge and figure out your project. Will you both accept my advice?"

Abby and Casey glanced at each other, then looked away.

"Okay, I guess," Abby said. It was better than fighting for the next three weeks.

Casey shrugged. "Why not? Hayes will squash all of *my* suggestions."

"No, I'll spinach them," Abby corrected.

Casey started to laugh.

"Why don't you study hamsters?" Bethany chirped. "They're a fascinating subject."

"No thanks," Abby said politely. Bethany's hamster did nothing but nibble, sleep, and scamper on a plastic wheel. She wasn't exactly a pet with personality.

"I've got it!" Natalie cried. "Why don't you put a rock collection together?"

"Rocks are my friends," Casey announced.

"He has them in his head," Abby murmured.

"You can go around to different places, like the quarry or the lake or the schoolyard, and find different rocks," Natalie explained. "Then you can display them with a report on where you found them and how they were formed."

"Do it," Bethany urged. "It's easy. It'll be fun."

"It's a good idea. If Hayes doesn't brain me with a boulder," Casey said.

Abby's friends looked at her expectantly.

She scuffed her toe in the gravel. She wouldn't have to speak to Casey until they had collected all the rocks. And they could start working now.

"Oh, all right," she said. "It's not very exciting. But I'll do it."

"Aaachooo!" Casey said. "Now that we've agreed on a science project, I better go take some medicine for my Hayes fever. Aaaaachooo!"

Bethany giggled.

"He's kind of cute," Natalie said as Casey walked away. "I think he likes you, Abby. I mean as a friend."

"Ugh! No way!" Abby cried. Casey was the worst boy she had ever met. He was worse than Zach, Tyler, and Mason combined. "I'll never be friends with *him*!"

Chapter 5

Thursday after school

"Nothing ever becomes real until it is experienced."
— John Keats

Alien Abduction Calendar

Like the haircut I'm going to get in forty-five minutes. I can't wait until I experience it!

My Horrid Hayes Hair has been all too real. I hope that Jeannie can fix it. My mom says she's a genius with hair. It better be true!

Change of subject! I don't want to think about my hair until it's time to get it cut. I will write a play instead.

<u>Playground Plays</u>
by Abby Hayes

Abby sees Brianna and Bethany on the playground. She goes over to them. In her hand is a tube of Brianna's Best Hair Gel. She gives it to Brianna.

Abby: Thanks.

Brianna: It helps, doesn't it.

Abby: Yes. I'm getting my hair cut later today. <u>Finally.</u>

Brianna: Jacques cuts my hair.

Abby: Zhock?

Brianna: Jacques. <u>Il est français. Tu comprends, n'est-ce pas?</u>

Abby: Nest paws?

Brianna: It's French. So is Jacques. He's the best. He has an autographed picture of me on his wall. I'd never allow anyone else to cut my hair.

Bethany: Yay, Brianna.

Brianna preens and struts. Bethany cheers and admires. A fifth grader from Mrs. McMillan's class, Victoria, joins the group.

Victoria (excited): Brianna, I have, like, an awesome idea for our, like, science project, like, you'll never believe. It's, like, so cool. It's the best!

Brianna (excited): I asked my mother if you could come to dinner tonight. She said yes.

Victoria (excited): Awesome.

Bethany (not excited): Brianna, we were supposed to Rollerblade –

Victoria: She's, like, made other plans!

Brianna: I'm not in the mood to Rollerblade.

Victoria and Brianna link arms and walk away.

Abby (tries to cheer Bethany up): I, like, think, like, Victoria, is, like, not, like, that, like, awesome, you know?

Bethany doesn't smile.

Behind her, Casey Hoffman is making faces. Abby turns around and sees him.

Abby: You don't have a part in this play!

Casey: Awwwww!

Abby: It's bad enough having to be your

science fair partner! Now you're showing up here!

Casey: Don't blow your stack, Hayes. <u>Hayes stack</u>. Get it?

Abby: Make like a needle and disappear.

Casey: Ha, ha, ha.

Abby signals the remaining actors, who exit offstage.

She writes "The End" in large, purple letters. Casey vanishes. She smiles and puts down her pen.

The Absolute, Final, Utter End

Dad just knocked on my door. He reminded me that in ten minutes he's driving me to Shear Delight for my haircut.

"I didn't forget!" I told him. "I've only been waiting for this appointment for an entire week. That's seven days, nine hours, and forty-two minutes."

"Okay, okay," Dad said. "I get the idea." He checked his watch. "Be downstairs in nine minutes and twenty-three seconds!"

✽   ✽   ✽

I must stop writing. I must stop writing now. I must put on my sneakers and take all the barrettes out of my hair. I promise to report back as soon as I get home from Shear Delight!

Thursday evening:

The Hair-raising Tale of a Trim

Jeannie, the hair-genius, whistled when she saw me.

"Wow," she said. "Your own mother did this?!"

"Yep," I said.

She led me over to the sink and shampooed my hair. Then she applied conditioner that smelled like bananas and straw-berries.

"My hair smells good enough to eat," I said as she rinsed off the conditioner.

"It already looks like someone chewed on

it," Jeannie commented as she led me to a big leather chair.

I sat in front of a wall of mirrors. Jeannie pulled on the strands of wet hair. "Shall we go short?" she asked.

"No!" I cried. "I don't want to look like a boy."

"You won't," she promised me. She combed out my hair. "I'll give you a bob."

"What's that?"

"It'll be around your chin. Not too short. But not long, either. You've already cut a lot off."

"Okay," I said nervously. "As long as it looks better than now."

Jeannie laughed. "Don't worry about that!"

Curls of wet hair fell to the floor as Jeannie snipped and clipped.

"Why is it called a bob?" I asked. "Why not a steve or a jonathan or a zeke? Why would a haircut be named after a boy?"

"Don't know," Jeannie said. She spritzed my hair and trimmed some more.

"Do you have an objective eye?" I asked. "That's what my mother said before she started cutting."

"I have a diploma from beautician school." Jeannie scrunched my hair with her hands. "Let your hair air-dry and don't use a blow-dryer. Otherwise you'll wreck all your curls."

"I hate them!" I groaned.

"Your hair is gorgeous," Jeannie said. "It's to die for."

"It's to die _from_," I mumbled. "Especially this last week."

She handed me a mirror. "What do you think?"

"Okay." I didn't want to look.

"Just _okay_?" She gestured to my father. "Come here and take a look at her!"

"Wow!" my father said as he joined us.

Jeannie nodded in agreement.

"_Cute_," my father said, handing her some folded-up bills.

The other customers smiled. My face turned red. Only now I had less of my hair to match it.

Jeannie gave me samples of the straw-berry-and-banana shampoo and conditioner.

"Stay away from those scissors!" she warned as we left. "Don't let your mother near them, either."

Dad took me out for ice cream. We talked about rocks. He said Alex got a bag of rocks for his birthday from his friend Collin.

I didn't know that! (Is it possible to live in the same house with siblings and miss important facts about them?)

Note to self: Be extra nice to little brother. Set table at dinner, even if it's his turn. Don't complain when he hogs computer. Pretend dumb cartoons are exciting.

Gently suggest that he lend me his rock collection for my science fair project.

When I got home, I looked at myself in the mirror.

"Bob" isn't too bad. (That's what I'm going to call my haircut.) It's shorter than

I usually wear it, but it's not _too_ short. It curls around my face. Jeannie said I don't have to fuss with it.

"Wash it and wear it," she said. "Just like a T-shirt."

Jeannie did a good job. She _is_ a hair-cutting genius. I bet she's better than Jacques. Will Brianna be jealous when she sees "Bob" tomorrow?

The horrible haircut nightmare is _over_! Hooray! Hooray! Run fingers lightly through hair. Skip around bedroom. Call friends! Arrange for group photograph.

Chapter 6

Saturday | morning

"A rolling stone gathers no moss."

Avalanche Calendar

Neither does one in a drawer.

That's where Alex keeps his collection, in a blue pouch with a drawstring. None of his stones or rocks has gathered moss. (Why would they gather moss, anyway?)

He has pitted yellow rocks, green sparkly ones, blue-veined ones, clear pink, and shiny black ones. He says I can borrow them for my science fair project, as long as I take good care of them.

That should make things easy!

Except it doesn't.

* * *

Problem #1: We have to find most of the rocks ourselves. We have to keep a journal of where we find them, what plants and animals live nearby, and how they were formed.

It's not scientific if we only use Alex's collection and don't do any fieldwork. Or if we go to the Science Museum and buy the rocks.

That's what Ms. Kantor said.

Okay, I see her point. We're not supposed to buy a science project. Or have it given to us, ready-made.

But . . .

Problem #2: The rocks in my yard are boring. There's no calcite, fluorite, apatite, autunite, chlorite, hematite, molybdenite, orpiment, azurite, malachite, eclogite, kyanite, halite, pyrite, gypsum, or aphthitalite.

(Writing this is making me lose my apatite!)

There are no sapphires, rubies, diamonds,

basalt, tourmaline, amber, garnets, amethysts, zircon, turquoise, or topaz.

There isn't even any sandstone, limestone, or marble!

All I could find was gray rocks! They're all alike! (Did a colony of them settle in my neighborhood? Did they get rid of the different-looking rocks?) This is going to be the worst, most boring science exhibit in the world! I can't believe I agreed to do it.

"Rocks" by Abby Hayes and Casey Hoffman. Gray rock found at bottom of garden. Gray pebble from driveway. Gray stone under porch. Gray . . .

Aaaaaahhhhhhhhh!!!

Problem #3: Casey invited me to search for rocks today. Jessica and Natalie are getting together with <u>their</u> partners. So are a lot of other people. He asked me in front of all my friends. I couldn't say no. He is coming to my house in only an hour. We are going to the park to look for rocks.

I have to spend the day with Casey Hoffman!

AAAAAAAAAAAAAAHHHHHHH! This

journal entry ends with a bloodcurdling scream.

"Let's walk toward the pond," Casey suggested. "I bet we find a lot of good stuff there."

"Okay," Abby said reluctantly. "I guess." She adjusted the straps of her backpack and hoisted it on her back.

The backpack held a notebook, pens, and guidebooks. It held a magnifying glass, labels, and plastic bags for sorting rocks. There was also a pocketknife and a microscope.

There was so much equipment, Abby wondered if the rocks would fit in!

"I hope this backpack is big enough," she said.

Alex pulled out a red nylon bag. "We can put lots of rocks in here."

"In Mom's laundry bag?" Abby exclaimed. "What are you thinking, Alex? It'll rip! It'll get filthy! Mom will be furious!"

"No, it won't rip! And Mom won't notice, anyway!" he protested. "Dad does most of the wash."

"Oh, yeah?" Abby said. "Besides, you won't be able to lug it home once it's full of rocks."

Alex's face fell.

"We can put our plant specimens in it," Casey suggested. "They'll be light. They won't ruin the bag. You'll be able to carry it home."

"Really?" Alex asked, brightening.

"Yep," Casey said. "I bet Hayes forgot to bring a bag for the plants. Didn't you, Hayes?" he said to Abby.

"We're collecting plants, too?" Abby asked irritably. "Aren't rocks enough?"

"Don't you want to get extra credit, Hayes?" Casey asked her.

"You need it, Abby!" Alex reminded her.

Abby scowled at the two of them. The afternoon had barely begun and already it was going in the wrong direction.

At first, it had seemed like a stroke of genius to invite Alex to join them.

"You have to protect me from Casey," Abby told Alex before they left. "You're my bodyguard."

"I'll be your buddy-guard," Alex said.

"Glare ferociously at Casey," Abby instructed him. "Don't let him call me Hayes. Don't let him tease me about my hair."

"I won't," Alex said. "Or we'll tease him right back."

"Two Hayes against one Hoffman," Abby said. "That'll even things out."

"Don't worry, Abby, I'll take care of you!" Alex promised.

"You're the greatest, Alex!"

Abby ran to her room and found a free ice-cream coupon that she had earned for doing extra chores. "This is for you," she said to her little brother. "You're a pal!"

But whose pal was he?

Since the moment they met, Alex followed Casey everywhere, listened to every word he spoke, watched every move he made.

Casey was extremely friendly to her little brother, too. He praised his ideas. He listened to Alex's endless conversation about robots. He told Alex stories about his family.

Casey and Alex were acting like best buddies instead of worst enemies.

It was infuriating! It was shocking! It was —

"You got a haircut, Hayes," Casey said to Abby as they crossed the park.

"Abby calls it 'Bob,'" Alex announced. "She cut

her hair when she was sick and made a mess out of it."

"Traitor," Abby muttered under her breath.

Casey nodded. "When I was little, I screamed so much when my mother tried to cut my hair that she had to sneak into my room when I was sleeping. She'd snip at it in the dark with blunt scissors," he said. "In the morning, my hair would stick out at weird angles."

"Ha, ha!" Alex yelled.

Abby gazed straight ahead.

"I think there should be a funny haircut contest," Casey said. "The winners could march in a parade."

"Uh-huh!" Alex agreed.

They turned onto a narrow path that led through the woods. From time to time, Casey stooped to pick up a rock that caught his eye.

"Watch out, Alex, that's poison ivy," Casey warned him. "That shiny stuff with three leaves."

"Have you ever had poison ivy?" Alex asked him.

"Yes, and it's no fun," Casey replied. "It itches like crazy. My older sister had it on her feet. She couldn't walk because of the blisters. My mother had to carry her around for a week."

"I won't put poison ivy in the plant bag!" Alex promised.

"You better not," Abby said. "That's all I need — poison ivy." What with bad haircuts, obnoxious science project partners, and traitorous brothers, she had all the problems lately that one fifth grader could handle.

"Look, a frog!" Casey pointed to a bullfrog poised on the edge of a rock.

Alex rushed toward it. With a splash, it disappeared into the water.

"I used to catch those little tree toads about the size of a thumbnail," Casey began telling Alex.

Abby tried not to listen. Listening to Casey Hoffman go on and on wasn't her idea of an exciting afternoon. Especially when Alex was hanging on his every word.

The three of them emerged from the woods. The sun was shining on the tall grasses by the pond. Birds darted back and forth. A few people strolled or sat at the edge of the water.

"A rock!" Alex cried. He picked up a large flat stone with a marbled surface.

"There are lots of them," Abby grumbled. She wished that she were home. "Big deal."

"Thanks, Alex. This is a real find." Casey examined the rock, then opened his backpack to put it away.

He took out a package of cookies. "Want one, Hayes?" he asked Abby.

"No thanks." Abby turned away.

Casey shrugged. "That means more for me and Alex. Right, Alex?"

"Right, Casey!" Alex shouted.

"Some buddy-guard," Abby muttered.

"I'm going to catch a frog," Alex announced, his mouth still full of cookies. He kicked off his shoes and waded barefoot into the pond.

"Stay close to the shore!" Abby warned him.

"Don't worry, Hayes, I'm a great swimmer," Casey said. He crossed his arms over his chest.

"Why do boys always brag?" Abby said.

Casey grinned. "Because it's true. Why do girls always worry about their hair?"

"I *don't* always worry about my hair!" Abby cried. "That's *not* true!"

"Don't blow your stack, Hayes."

"That wasn't funny the first time you said it."

"My jokes get better with age," Casey replied.

"*You* don't!" Abby retorted.

"Ha, ha, ha," Casey said.

"Shouldn't we be working on our science project?" Abby reminded him. "Why don't you go sketch a rock?"

Casey pulled out a notepad and a stick of charcoal. "Great idea, Hayes. I planned to sketch the natural habitats." He handed her some plastic bags. "You can sort your rocks into these."

"Gee, thanks," Abby said. "I already brought some."

Casey snapped his fingers. "Name three categories of rocks."

"Metamorphic, igneous, and sedimentary," Abby recited. She had studied them the night before.

"Just checking to see if you were on your toes."

"Oh, yeah? Name two kinds of igneous rocks!"

"Um . . ." Casey scratched his head. "Granite and . . ."

"Wrong!" Abby cried triumphantly. "Intrusive and extrusive."

"I got a frog!" Alex yelled, running toward them with cupped hands.

"Awesome," Casey said. "Let me see."

"Do you know the structure of the earth?" Abby asked Casey.

He shook his head. "No, I don't." He turned to Alex. "That's a baby peeper, Alex."

"Ha!" Abby said. "I do! There's the crust, the solid mantle, the molten outer core, the solid inner core . . ."

"Shhh!" Alex said. "You're scaring my frog."

"We have to keep ahead of the facts," Abby lectured Casey. "Otherwise we won't get a good grade."

"Later, Hayes," Casey said, taking the frog from Alex. "This is important."

"So is *this*!" Abby retorted.

"*Ssshhhh!*" Alex said again.

Abby marched over to the pond.

"I gave up a free ice-cream coupon for *this*?" she fumed. "I should have left Alex at home with his robots!"

She could have endured a few hours of teasing from Casey, she told herself. That would have been nothing. She could have teased him right back. But watching Alex become friends with Casey was the worst!

It wasn't fair! Alex was supposed to confide in *her*, admire *her*, want to be with *her* . . .

Was she jealous of Casey Hoffman?

No — of course she wasn't. Casey was jealous of

her. She had a great little brother like Alex, while he had an older sister dumb enough to walk in poison ivy barefoot.

Abby smiled. She picked up some rocks. She would fill her pack while Casey was admiring the baby peeper. She would label and classify the rocks. The faster she got done, the sooner the afternoon would be over. She would take Alex home. He would never see Casey again.

Chapter 7

> Tuesday
>
> **"Those who do not complain are never pitied."**
>
> — *Jane Austen*
>
> **The Great Big Calendar of Sneezes**

I complained all day Sunday. No one pitied me at all. Why not????????

<u>Pathetic Events in the House of Hayes:</u>

1. As we were leaving the park, Alex invited Casey to our house.
2. Casey said yes. He stayed for the afternoon.
3. Mom invited Casey for dinner.
4. He sat at the table right next to me.
5. My entire family liked him.
6. He watched a movie with us.

7. Dad _finally_ drove him home at 9:00 p.m.

8. That adds up to eight whole hours of Casey Hoffman.

9. An overdose!!!! I have a bad case of too much Casey!

No one in my family pities me. No one attempts to understand my terrible ordeal. Not one single person. Not even the cat! Why not? Why not? Why not?

Mrs. McMillan's class and Ms. Kantor's class had gathered in the library to work on their science projects.

An excited buzz arose from the class. The students' materials were spread out over the tables. Victoria and Brianna were folding a pile of fashionable T-shirts. Crystal and Bethany argued about a hamster maze. Mason was blowing up balloons and popping them loudly. Jessica and Sarah discussed pollution. Natalie, Amanda, and Dylan examined the crystals they had grown.

Casey and Abby sorted through their rock collection. They had divided their collection into three sections: igneous, metamorphic, and sedimentary. They selected the best for display and threw out duplicates.

"How's 'Bob' today?" Casey teased as he compared two different specimens of sandstone. "Are you taking good care of him, Hayes?"

At the next table, Brianna looked up.

"Who's Bob?" she asked Abby. "Your boyfriend?"

"My haircut," Abby said. She picked up a polished piece of jasper and turned it over to examine it. It had come from Alex's collection.

Victoria frowned. "Like, why do you name your haircut?"

"Like, why not?" Abby glanced at Casey. He was grinning.

"That's a lot of T-shirts," Casey said to Victoria and Brianna. "Are you studying the science of shopping?"

"We have an even better idea," Brianna bragged. "We're comparing different brands of T-shirts. We have five categories: cost, appearance, durability, colorfastness, and shrinkage."

"Like, this is the coolest," Victoria said, holding

up an apple-green shirt. "I totally love this color, you know?"

"This one." Brianna held up a lace shirt. "If it shrinks in the wash, I'm going to buy another one. It's so totally cool."

"They need a Cool-o-Meter," Casey said under his breath.

If anyone but Casey had said it, Abby would have laughed. Instead she pointed to a piece of volcanic rock. "What's this?"

"That's from my sister Jamie. She got it in Hawaii."

"The sister with poison ivy?"

Casey nodded. "Look at this," he said. "I found rose quartz and fossils in my drawer. The fossils are from the lake."

"I'll write up the labels," Abby offered. She scribbled some notes on a piece of paper. "I'm also writing reports on how the three types of rocks are formed."

"Great, Hayes," Casey said. "With my pictures, we're bound to get a good grade. Wait until you see them. They'll knock your socks off!"

"I wish you'd knock off the bragging instead," Abby murmured.

Casey laughed. "You haven't seen my pictures. They'll change your mind!"

"Where do you, like, buy your socks?" Victoria asked Casey. "How, like, long before they, you know, get holes?"

"If you want to know about socks with holes, ask Alex," Casey said.

"Whose boyfriend is Alex?" Brianna demanded.

"He's in second grade," Casey said. "He's Abby's brother. And he has plenty of holes in his socks."

"His drawer is full of new ones," Abby explained quickly. She didn't want everyone to think that Alex went around with ripped clothing. "He just forgets to put them on."

"That sounds like Alex," Casey said.

"He's *my* little brother," Abby reminded him.

"You know Abby's family?" Brianna asked Casey.

Casey tossed a rock from one hand to another. "I had dinner with them on Saturday night."

"Oh," Brianna said. Her eyes widened. She glanced at Victoria.

"Alex invited him!" Abby said quickly.

"You don't need to hide it, Abby," Brianna said. "You should be proud of having a boyfriend."

"Yeah," Victoria breathed. "Like, I'd be telling *everyone*."

"He's *not* my boyfriend!" Abby cried. "He's not even a *friend*!"

Casey ducked his head.

"Who, like, cares?" Victoria said. "I mean, whether he is or isn't your friend or boyfriend, you know." She laughed.

"He's *not* my friend!" Abby repeated.

Casey looked away. His mouth curled down. He reached for the box of rocks and began to sort them.

Brianna and Victoria returned to comparing their T-shirts.

Her face flushed, Abby picked up a rock specimen and wrote a label for it. Then she labeled another.

"Class?" Ms. Kantor and Mrs. McMillan rang a bell at the desk to get everyone's attention.

"Start cleaning up your projects," they announced. "We're returning to our classrooms in ten minutes."

Casey emptied the rocks they didn't want into a large paper bag.

Abby sealed up the three boxes of sedimentary, igneous, and metamorphic rocks and their labels.

Neither of them spoke. Abby avoided Casey's eyes.

"Should I take these home?" she finally asked.

"Okay." He didn't look at her, either. "I'll get rid of the extras."

Mrs. McMillan rang the bell again. Without saying another word, Abby and Casey went to their separate classrooms.

Chapter 8

Wednesday

"I never apologize."
— *George Bernard Shaw*

Daily Excuse Calendar

When I quoted this to my family, they all disagreed!

Mom: Everyone makes mistakes. It's a sign of character to admit that you're wrong.

Eva: Not apologizing can ruin a friendship.

Alex: When someone hurts your feelings, it helps if they say "sorry."

Isabel: A little apology goes a long way.

Dad: "I'm sorry" are two of the most important words in the English language. Especially if they're sincere.

Abby: Is that true?

Entire family: YES!!!

I <u>don't</u> want to apologize to Casey Hoffman for anything!

But I think I'm going to have to. I've not only hurt his feelings, but I've done something much worse.

<u>News Report!</u>

At 3:15 p.m. on Tuesday, Abby Hayes, a fifth grader, walked home through the park. In her arms, she carried boxes of sedimentary, igneous, and metamorphic rocks. In her mind whirled furious thoughts about Casey Hoffman. She wished she had never met him. She wished she had another science partner. She wished —

"Abby! Abby!" It was Jessica, playing soccer with Sarah, the science partner she liked. "Come join us!" she called.

"We need a third player," Sarah added. She kicked the ball toward Abby.

Abby smiled.

"Just a minute!" she said. She carefully placed her rock collection under a tree. Then she ran into the field to join her friends.

The three girls played soccer for half an hour. Then —

We end the news report here.

The reporter doesn't want to report any more. The news is too painful to write. The reporter is too upset. Instead, she is going to whisper to her journal what happened next.

(I lost the rocks.)

I lost the rocks.

I lost the rocks!

I LOST THE ROCKS! (Okay, this is a shriek, not a whisper.)

Our science project is gone!

Dear Journal, you are probably wondering how I did something so dumb. Well, I played soccer with my friends, went to get a soda, and forgot all about the rocks. I went home, had dinner, started my homework – and remembered that I had left them at the park. Dad drove me back. He said we'd find them where I'd left them – under the tree. We didn't. They weren't there – or anywhere else.

What happened to my rocks? Where did they go? Who took them? Will I ever get them back? What will I do?

We pause for a moment of silent screaming.

Help, help, HELP! The entire collection is gone. All the rocks we collected at the pond, in our backyards, and at school have disappeared. Alex's collection is gone and so are the rocks that Casey's sister Jamie lent us.

And what about the science fair? We <u>have</u> to complete a project! It's part of our grade, even without the extra credit.

Casey will be SOOOO angry! (How many apologies will I have to make? At least a billion. That probably won't be enough.)

What else can I do? <u>Think!</u>

<u>Make Excuses to Casey:</u>
    a) The rocks went on strike.
    b) A UFO took them to their leader.
    c) The rocks entered a time warp and are now in the Jurassic Era.
    d) They defected to another school.
    e) A wizard needed them for his experiments and I couldn't say no.

<u>Problems with Excuses:</u>
    (Obvious)

<u>Other Plans of Action:</u>
    a) Throw myself on Casey Hoffman's mercy.

b) Put together a second rock collection exactly like the first.

c) Pretend there never <u>was</u> a rock collection.

d) Leave town for a year or two.

e) Blame it on the dog.

<u>Problems with Other Plans of Action:</u>

a) Hoffman will have no mercy on Hayes!

b) I can't <u>remember</u> what was in the first rock collection.

c) Yeah, right.

d) Never mind.

e) What dog?

Even Better Plans:

Be practical. Think of a solution. Don't be afraid.

There is always an answer. That's what my mother says.

What is it? I need to know <u>NOW</u>!

Chapter 9

Thursday

"Leave no stone unturned."

— *Euripides*

Garden Tractor Calendar

We didn't.

Dad, Eva, Isabel, and I went to the park again last night to look for the rock collection.

We looked everywhere. Even in the water. Even in trees. Even in trash cans. We didn't find it.

We asked park employees if they had seen it. We asked Rollerbladers. We asked mothers and babies. We asked grandfathers and skateboarders.

We asked dog-walkers and kids with purple hair.

No one had seen the rock collection.

I asked Dad and twin genius sisters what to do.

"Tell Casey," they all said.

"Don't you have another answer?" I asked.

They didn't.

Why did I worry so much about my haircut? That was nothing compared to this! I'd rather go to school bald than tell Casey Hoffman the truth!

I might have to. Tell Casey Hoffman the truth, I mean.

(Maybe I should shave my head. . . . If I was bald, no one would remember the rock collection.)

Dad, Eva, and Isabel all promised not to say anything to Alex — for a while.

"You'll have to replace his collection," Dad said to me.

"Okay," I promised.

That'll be easy — especially compared to the rest of what I have to do.

Time is running out. My class is meeting his class this afternoon. Casey expects me to bring our project. What am I going to tell him? This is the worst moment of my life!

As Ms. Kantor's class filed down the hallway, Abby clutched her binder and rehearsed what she was going to say to Casey.

"I left it at home . . . We can work on it later . . . I don't know where it is."

That last one, at least, was true.

Abby groaned. She had had butterflies in her stomach all day. There were probably wasps, bees, and mosquitoes there, too. Even creative writing hadn't cheered her up. Her favorite subject with her favorite teacher had tortured her the way math usually did.

Ms. Bunder had asked the class to describe their favorite place and what it meant to them.

All Abby had been able to write was "My favorite place is anywhere but here." She had crumpled her paper into a ball and thrown it in the garbage.

Ms. Bunder had looked at her in surprise but didn't say anything. Abby didn't explain.

At recess, Abby had stayed in. She didn't want to encounter Casey Hoffman. Her friends went outside. Ms. Kantor talked with Ms. Yang, the principal. Abby stayed alone in the classroom.

Now, as the class walked to the library, Abby hoped to talk to her friends. But they were all engaged in other conversations.

Natalie was deep in a discussion of hamsters with Bethany.

Jessica was already in the library. She was looking up information on the Web. She and Sarah were planning an overnight trip for the weekend. They were going to observe the stars in the country *and* the city and see where they shone brightest.

Mason and Zach were talking about inventing a Burp-o-scope for an extra-credit science fair project.

"Let's rate burps like earthquakes!" Zach suggested.

"I'll be first to test it out." Mason burped loudly. "That's an eight on the Mason-Zach scale!" he shouted.

"Quiet!" Ms. Kantor warned.

Brianna was surrounded by a group of girls. She

was telling them how she had modeled for a cream-cheese commercial.

Abby wished she could turn into a block of cream cheese. Or even cottage cheese. As they got closer to the library, her heart began to thud violently. Her face flushed. Her stomach cramped. Maybe she was getting sick again?

She sat down in the nearest chair while her classmates hurried to meet their partners from the other class.

Brianna and Victoria greeted each other with loud cries. "It's so, like, great to see you!" Victoria cried. "It's been, like, hours since recess!"

"I have the best T-shirts," Brianna said. "I brought five more."

Natalie, Amanda, and Dylan gathered at a table and unpacked supplies.

Bethany hammered at the hamster maze. Her partner, Crystal, handed her the nails — though she dropped most of them.

"What's the matter?" Ms. Kantor asked Abby. "Why aren't you working on your project?"

"I'm waiting for Casey," Abby mumbled. "He's not here yet."

"Get going!" Ms. Kantor said. "The science fair is only a week away."

Abby took a deep breath. "Ms. Kantor, I lost it," she said. Her voice shook a little. "I lost my science fair project. I left it in the park and it disappeared."

Her teacher frowned. "That's too bad, Abby. But you'll still have to do it over."

"I can't!" Abby cried.

Ms. Kantor shook her head. "Then you'll have to start a new project. Unless you want a failing grade."

Tears came into Abby's eyes.

"You'll find some ideas in here!" Ms. Kantor pointed to a library shelf with a display of science titles. "You can do it if you get started now. You don't have a moment to lose!"

Abby slowly walked over to the books and began flipping through the pages. Some of the projects looked too complicated; others looked too boring. Besides, Casey would never like anything she liked.

If he had been obnoxious before, Casey was going to be *impossible* once he found out that she had lost their science project!

Abby took a deep breath. She wished she could fast-forward in time. She wished it was next year already.

"Hi, Hayes!"

"Hi." Abby darted a quick look at Casey face. How should she begin? "Uh, hi," she said a

"How's Bob?" Casey asked in a friendly way.

"Bob is wild," she answered. Maybe they could talk about her hair instead of the rock collection.

Casey grinned at her. "Glad to hear it. Where are we sitting?"

"Over there."

He went to the table and unpacked a set of drawings. "Come on, let's start. Where are the rocks?"

Abby's heart thudded. She couldn't sit down. "Those are nice drawings," she said.

"I knew you'd like them!" Casey said triumphantly. "Let's put them with the rocks and see how good they look together."

"Um, can we wait?" Abby said.

"Why?" Casey asked.

"Uh . . ." The room began to whirl around her. She put her hand on her forehead. Was she getting a fever? Was she going to faint?

"What's the matter?" Casey asked. "You okay?"

Abby took a breath. It was now or never.

"I lost the rocks," she whispered.

"You *what*?" Casey said.

"I lost the rocks!" she cried. "They're gone!"

Chapter 10

Thursday still

"The unexpected always
happens."

-Swiss Watch Calendar

YES! (It's true.)

I told Casey the whole story. Everything.
Once I began to talk, I couldn't stop. I
told him about the soccer game, forgetting
the rocks, going back to look for them twice,
and realizing the collection was lost forever.
  Finally, I was done. I stopped and
looked at Casey.

I didn't expect to tell him everything.
And I didn't expect his reaction, either.

*   *   *

 He was frowning. His mouth was shut and he was gazing in the distance. He didn't say a word.

"If you're mad," Abby said, "I don't blame you at all. I'm so sorry."

Casey stared at Abby for a moment. Then he shook his head. "I can't believe you, Hayes."

"What do you mean?"

"You organized a search party and everything."

"So?"

"You should have called me!" Casey said. "I would have helped you."

Abby gaped at him. "You would have?"

"Sure."

"You wouldn't have been mad?"

"Naw. I lose things all the time. Socks, money, Rollerblades. It drives my mom crazy."

"This is worse than a sock. I lost your sister's volcanic rock from Hawaii," Abby pointed out. "Won't *she* be mad?"

Casey didn't say anything.

Abby shook her head. What was it with him? Didn't he get it? Didn't he understand what she had done?

"We have to redo our science project. That means starting all over again."

"We'll figure something out," he said. "Our two great brains will come up with an award-winning idea."

"Yeah, right," Abby said. "Two heads are better than one."

They exchanged glances.

"Have you told Alex?" Casey asked, after a moment. "Was he upset?"

"Not yet," Abby said. "I'm going to the Science Museum later today to replace his collection."

She patted her pocket. She had brought $18.76 to school. She hoped it was enough.

"I hope I can remember what was in the collection," she added. "I tried to make a list this morning, but — "

"I'll help you, Hayes," Casey offered.

"Thanks . . . Hoffman."

Casey and Abby looked at each other. Then they looked away.

He took out a piece of paper. "We better start thinking about what we're going to do next."

"Right," Abby agreed.

"More rocks?" Casey suggested.

Abby frowned. "How? We can't replace our collection in a couple of days! We'd have to collect it, sort it, label it . . ."

"Yeah . . ." Casey flipped through his drawings. "It's just a shame to lose all this work."

"I did a lot of work, too. I wrote up a report about how rocks are formed." Abby pulled out three typewritten pages.

"Maybe we can use our work in another project."

"Oh, yeah? *What?*" Abby demanded. "A demonstration of the rocks in my head? How to lose your rocks *and* your marbles at the same time?"

"That's pretty funny, Hayes."

"Ha, ha," Abby said. "I wish I was as good at coming up with projects as I am with jokes."

She glanced around the room. Everyone else was busy with their projects. They were making charts and graphs. They were building mazes and growing crystals. They were measuring, comparing, and observing.

Only she and Casey were back at square one.

"We better think of an easy project fast," Casey said. "Or we won't have one at all."

"Volcanoes?" Abby suggested.

"Two kids in my class are doing them. How about proving yawns are contagious?"

"Ho hum," Abby said. "How about making home-made perfumes?"

"That's a girl project, Hayes."

"Are we going to fight about this again, Hoffman?" Abby said. "We don't have time to argue."

"You're right," Casey agreed. "Let's write down our ideas on a piece of paper and then we'll choose the best one."

"Okay . . ." Abby agreed. She pulled out a fresh sheet of paper and her journal.

Ideas for Easy Science Fair Project:
1.
2.
3.
4.

Uh-oh! I can't think of anything! Casey is staring at his paper, too. What are we going to do? How will I ever get extra credit? Forget about extra credit. How will I get a passing grade?

Must stop worrying and start thinking!

<u>Thoughts:</u>

1. Casey was pretty nice about my losing the rocks.

2. He's not that bad.

3. I don't mind him calling me "Hayes."

4. He gets all my jokes.

5. He's . . .

Must stop thinking and start worrying!

<u>More Ideas:</u>

1. Show how —

Help! Mrs. McMillan and Ms. Kantor just told us to put away our work. It's time to go back to our classrooms.

Casey showed me his blank page. I showed him my empty page.

Zero plus zero equals zero. Will that be our science project? Show how nothing comes out of nothing?

No, that will be our grade if we don't figure out what we're doing <u>soon</u>!

Chapter 11

Thursday still

"Man is able to do what he
is unable to imagine."

— Rene Char

Flying Acrobat Calendar

So is Girl!

A few hours ago I would have been unable to imagine going to the Science Museum with Casey Hoffman. Or having a friendly conversation with him.

I did both those things — and more!

We went to the Museum Store and bought a blue drawstring bag for Alex just like his old one. Then we went over to the rock display and filled it with rocks. Casey helped me pick out the ones that Alex had.

They weren't like the rocks I found in my backyard – gray and boring! They were clear, pink, rose, blue, black, green, yellow, purple, marbled, shiny, dull, heavy, light, flat, and round.

"Too bad we can't use these for our project," I said to Casey, as I picked up a photocopied sheet telling their names and where they were found.

"Ms. Kantor and Mrs. McMillan said we had to do fieldwork," he said.

"We _did_ fieldwork, didn't we?" I sighed. "But I lost it. Maybe we can do a scientific study about disappearance."

"Great idea, Hayes!" Casey cried. "Where do socks go? They're always disappearing. Where do coins and buttons go? What happens to all the things that are never found?"

"Like our rocks!" I said. "Maybe I could do a survey of lost objects."

"With charts and graphs!"

"We'll interview the whole neighborhood!" I gestured with my hand. "We'll use a tape recorder and take pictures and – "

Casey interrupted me. "There are only five days until the science fair."

Both of us fell silent.

"Another brilliant idea hits the dust," I said sadly.

"Sorry, Hayes," Casey said.

I put the drawstring bag on the counter and pulled out my money.

"That'll be $13.51," the woman at the cash register said as she counted the rocks I had put in the bag.

I handed her the money. There was $5.25 left.

"Wait a minute!" I raced back to the display, picked up a few more items, and returned to the register.

"These, too, please," I said to the woman.

She put my purchases in a bag and handed them to me. "Enjoy your rocks."

"I wish I could," I said.

"At least Alex will," Casey said.

<u>More Unimaginable Things That "Girl"</u>
<u>Was Able to Do:</u>
Walk home with Casey Hoffman!
(Thank goodness no one saw us.)
Invite him into my house.
(Yes, I did.)
Show him my calendars!
(This is for real! I'm not making this
up!)

Casey left. Then Alex came home. I told
him what had happened.
(His reaction was not "unexpected" like
Casey's.)
"You lost my collection?" he yelled. "The
one that Collin gave me for my birthday?"
"I'm sorry!" I said. "I didn't do it on
purpose!"
Alex kept on yelling. "I told you to take
good care of it!"
"I'm <u>sorry!</u>" I said again. "I bought you
a new one to replace it."
"It's not the same." Alex folded his arms
across his chest and glared at me. "I'll
never forgive you, Abby."

I glared back. "It's <u>exactly</u> like the one that was lost."

"It can't be!" Alex insisted.

"Casey said so."

"Casey?" Alex's voice suddenly changed. "When did he see it?"

"He helped me pick out the rocks."

"Casey helped you?" Alex repeated. "He was here?"

I nodded.

"Why didn't you <u>tell</u> me he was coming over!" Alex cried. He was mad again.

"I didn't know!"

Alex gave me another look. "Show me the rocks," he ordered.

I handed him the blue pouch. He opened it up and took out the rocks. He examined each one of them. Then he put them back into the pouch.

"This is all right," he said. "It's close enough."

I breathed a sigh of relief. (Note: why not a cough of relief? Or a whisper of relief? Or a huff of relief?) Okay, I nearly choked with relief!

"When is Casey coming over again?" Alex demanded. "I want to see him!"

"This weekend. We have to figure out a new science project and do the whole thing in less than a week."

"Robots?" Alex suggested. "I'll help you both."

"No thanks." I picked up my journal. "Go away, Alex. I want to be alone."

"Tell Casey I like the rock collection."

"Casey, Casey, Casey!" I cried. "What is it with him?"

Five minutes later. Alex is gone. I am left with many questions.

Question: Is "Casey" a magic word? Alex would not have accepted the new rock collection without it.

Saying "Casey" transformed my little brother from furious to curious.

(Will it work on other members of the Hayes family? Must try at soonest possible opportunity.)

Another question: Why does my little

brother like Casey Hoffman so much?

Alex acts like Casey is the
sun, the moon, and the stars.
All he wants to do is revolve
around him.

Casey is <u>okay</u>. He's not as
bad as I thought. He's even nice sometimes. Well, once in a while. I don't want
to get <u>too</u> friendly with Casey Hoffman.

Like my mother says, "This is strictly
business!"

As soon as we're done with our science
project, that's it! I'm not going to hang
around with Casey any longer than I have
to.

Imagine what my friends and classmates
would say if I became good friends with
a boy!

Brianna: Abby has a boyfriend.

Victoria: Abby has, like, a boyfriend, you
know.

Mason: Abby has a boyfriend. (Burps a

ten-and-a-half on the Mason-Zach scale.)

Jessica: You have a <u>boyfriend</u>?

Natalie: "Did you say <u>boy</u> friend?"

(This is getting boring. It wouldn't be boring if it actually happened, though. It would be <u>horrible!</u>)

No, no, <u>no</u>! It won't happen!

After the science project is finished, I won't invite Casey to my house ever again. I won't show him my calendars. I won't ask him to help me pick out rocks for Alex.

I will spend my free time with Jessica and Natalie. And Bethany, too (if she stops talking so much about hamsters). We will play soccer together, have sleepovers, and talk about Brianna.

I will say hello to Casey in hallways and at recess. I will joke with him. Once in a while I might even throw a ball to him. But that's <u>it</u>!

Another question: Why is it so awful for

a girl to be friends with a boy? (This has nothing to do with Casey. Really!)

Suppose a girl and boy just like each other. As friends only. Why does everyone have to tease them?

I want to know!!!

One final question: Why am I writing so much about a boy????

Chapter 12

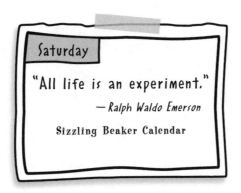

Then it ought to be easy to figure out a science fair project!

It _is_ easy to find a project if you look in the library. Casey and I took out six books of science experiments. There were <u>hundreds</u> of projects! We wrote down a list of our favorites:

1. Make a battery out of a lemon. (Then take a ride in your lemon mobile.)

2. Model how people imagined the universe in

the past and present. (People used to think the world was flat!)

3. Show how first-, second-, and third-class levers work. (This project will give you a lift.)

4. Find the parts of a bean. (Easy!)

5. Use a blender to show how igneous rocks are made. In real life, they're made from volcanoes and lava. Then show how pressure and layers turn them into sedimentary rock. (This experiment rocks! Ha, ha, ha. It really does.)

Casey found it. He pointed out that if we do this experiment, we can use our research, too!

Hooray! Hooray! Hooray! We started last night because it takes a couple of days for the "rocks" to form.

All we had to do was blend a bunch of construction paper in the blender with water and glue.

Then we strained the water and put our rocks on newspaper to dry. It will take only a couple of days.

We'll combine our new experiment with the old report and drawings. I bet Ms. Kantor and Mrs. McMillan will like it. Maybe I'll even get a good grade in science!

Abby dribbled the basketball down the driveway, stopped, and threw it at the basket.

The ball bounced off the rim.

"You need more follow-through," Eva said. "Like this." She picked up the ball and swished it into the basket.

Abby frowned and tried again. The ball ricocheted off the backboard. "I just can't get it," she complained.

"Try again," Eva encouraged her. She effortlessly made another basket, then passed the ball to Abby.

Abby threw the ball. It wobbled on the rim, then plunged into the hoop.

"Basket!" Abby cried. "I did it!"

"Way to go!" Eva said. She checked her watch. "I've got to get ready for softball practice now. Keep it up, Abby."

Eva hurried into the house. Abby's next shot didn't even hit the basketball hoop. Nor did the next.

"I'm not keeping it up," Abby muttered to herself.

Maybe Eva was her lucky charm. Maybe her athletic ability rubbed off on Abby. Unfortunately, it disappeared when Eva did.

The ball rolled into the grass. Abby didn't run after it.

She sat down on the back steps. Eva had softball practice; Isabel was at a play rehearsal; Alex was playing with a friend. Her mother was shopping and her father was in his home office.

She went into the house to get the phone. It seemed like weeks since she had seen Jessica outside of school.

"Is this Jessica? Hi, it's Abby."

"Hi." Jessica was laughing. "Just a minute." She covered the receiver with her hand. Then she came back on the line. "What's up?"

"Do you want to Rollerblade in the park?" Abby asked.

"Sarah's here," Jessica said. "We're putting the finishing touches on our report."

"Maybe afterward?" Abby suggested.

There was a pause.

"We're having a sleepover," Jessica said. "So I can't."

"Oh." Abby took a breath. "Well, have a good time."

"Thanks," Jessica said.

Sarah said something that Abby couldn't make out.

"Gotta go now!" Jessica said. "See you!"

Abby hung up the phone. She dialed again. "Hello? Is Natalie there?"

"Natalie!" her father called.

Abby waited.

"Natalie!" he called again. "Just a minute," he said to Abby. "I think she's in her room." He put down the phone.

Abby stared at a spiderweb on the ceiling. She heard Natalie's father going up the stairs and then coming back down again.

"Natalie is at Bethany's. She'll be back after dinner."

"Okay, thanks," Abby said. "You can tell her I called."

She sat with the phone in her lap. No reason to

call Bethany. She was with Natalie. Her closest friends were all busy. Now what could she do?

Call Casey? No. She couldn't. He was a boy.

But who else was there? Brianna?

"I must be crazy," she muttered to herself. "Or truly desperate. But at least she's a girl." She dialed Brianna's number.

"Hi, Abby," Brianna said. She sounded friendly.

"Want to Rollerblade in the park?" Abby asked.

"I'd love to," Brianna said. "But Victoria is here. We're going shopping. Want to join us?"

"Sure," Abby said. The words were out of her mouth before she could think about them. "Where?"

"At the mall. My mom can pick you up in half an hour."

"I'll ask my dad." She put down the phone and ran up the stairs. Then she ran back down.

"He said yes," Abby said to Brianna.

"Awesome," Brianna said. "Bring your credit card."

"I don't have one," Abby said.

"You don't have charge accounts?" Brianna asked impatiently. "How about a debit card?"

"Um, no. I'll bring my allowance."

"Victoria and I are going on a spree," Brianna said. "We're buying earrings, purses, and colored lip gloss."

"If I empty my penny jar, I'll have enough money for a chocolate pretzel," Abby said. She said good-bye and hung up the phone.

"I *must* be crazy," she said to herself. "Crazy, crazy, crazy."

Was going shopping with Brianna and Victoria *really* better than spending the afternoon alone? Or with Casey? Why had he been so nice about losing the rocks? It was much easier to hate him!

"Let's go in that store," Victoria said. "It's got, like, the most totally awesome face glitter. It's, like, the best."

"They've got cool things," Brianna agreed.

Abby tagged behind the two girls. They had been in the mall only fifteen minutes and already Brianna and Victoria had bought bracelets, anklets, and hair ornaments.

Brianna picked up a plastic purse with tubes of lip gloss inside. "Aren't these cute?"

Victoria made a face. "They're, like, for little kids."

"What do you think?" Brianna asked Abby.

Abby shrugged. "I'm not a purse person. Purse-son. Get it?" She made a mental note to say that to Casey. He'd think it was funny.

Brianna and Victoria didn't.

"These purses are cute," Brianna insisted.

"Like, okay. Don't, like, get all upset and, like, strange about it."

"I'm going to buy one," Brianna said. "I'll start a new fad."

"Like, who cares?" Victoria said nastily.

Brianna tossed her hair over her shoulder. "I'm number one! I take French lessons, act in commercials, ride horses, and sing onstage! *Moi, je parle français. Je suis très belle!*"

"Bell?" Victoria sneered. "Dingdong!"

"I'm a star!" Brianna cried. "I'm the most popular girl in the fifth grade."

"*I* am the most popular," Victoria said. "I mean, it's *me*."

"*You?*" Brianna retorted. "I don't think so!"

Victoria turned red. "You're so, like, you know, like, I mean, so, so, *like* — " she sputtered.

Suddenly she turned to Abby. "You decide!" she said. "Which of us is the most popular?"

"Um . . ." Abby scrambled to think of the right thing to say. If she chose one over the other, she was in trouble. If she said nothing, she was in trouble. Whatever she did, she was doomed.

"Can't you both be the most popular?" she asked.

"No!!" they yelled in unison.

"Or take turns?" Abby suggested.

"This isn't nursery school," Brianna said impatiently.

"Like, you can't expect us to share," Victoria snapped. "It's so, like, babyish."

"So who is it?" Brianna said. "Me or Victoria?"

Abby glanced at the clock on the wall. Forty-five minutes before Brianna's mom showed up. "Um," she said again.

"Well?" Victoria demanded. "We're waiting for your answer."

Abby took a breath. She felt as if she were trapped in a jar with two wasps. How could she keep them from stinging her?

"This is too important for just one person to decide," she finally said. "You need to ask more people!"

Brianna raised her arms skyward. "The people shall speak!"

"Everyone in the school should, like, vote on it," Victoria agreed.

"We'll hire an independent polling company."

"Or, like, a private investigator."

Abby edged toward the door. "I'm going to get a pretzel," she told them. "I'll be back in fifteen minutes."

"Don't, like, get lost or anything," Victoria told her.

"My mother hates to wait!" Brianna warned.

Abby found a bench outside the store, then pulled out her journal and began to write.

<u>Phew!</u> That was close! Good thing I thought of telling them that one person shouldn't make such an "important" decision.

Good thing there's a pretzel shop nearby.

Good thing they're so busy discussing the popularity contest, they don't care if I leave!

Who is worse? Brianna or Victoria?

Compared to Victoria, Brianna is nice.
Compared to Brianna, Victoria is modest.
Compared with Casey, they're both awful.
Even though they're both girls.

This afternoon of shopping will go down
in history as the "Mall Maul." I will
make the <u>Hayes Book of World Records</u> as
"Only Known Lone Survivor of Brianna-
Victoria Shopping Spree." (I <u>hope</u> I survive.
There are still twenty-eight minutes and fifteen seconds left.)

How many arguments will Brianna and
Victoria have in the next half hour? (hundreds)
How many bags of jewelry, makeup, and
clothing will they buy? (dozens)
How many times will Victoria say, "like,
you know?" (billions)
How many times will Abby wish she had invited Casey Hoffman to her house? (no comment)

An afternoon with Casey would have
been a breeze!

Why a breeze? Why not a zephyr, gentle wind, or a draft?

Okay, an afternoon with Casey Hoffman would have been a zephyr! (He would think that's funny.)

This afternoon with Brianna and Victoria is a tornado, a typhoon, and a monsoon. (They wouldn't think that's funny!)

Only twenty-five minutes and twelve seconds left.

I am killing time. Why kill time? Why not pass it, like a car on a highway? I'd like to zoom ahead at eighty miles an hour to tonight.

Uh-oh. Here come Victoria and Brianna. They are smiling and laughing. They are friends again. They have six new bags of "cool stuff."

Chapter 13

Sunday

"The next day is never so good as the day before."

— *Publius Syrus*

Daily Grind Calendar

Wrong! Today was <u>much</u> better than yesterday!

Today I invited Casey over. (All my friends were <u>still</u> busy! Jessica was at Sarah's. Natalie was with her family. Bethany was at Brianna's.)

It was fun having Casey here. Especially after spending the afternoon with Brianna and Victoria.

I don't know which was worse, their arguments or their agreements!

❋   ❋   ❋

Their arguments:
(You know about them!)

Their agreements:
Brianna: Where did you get those awesome earrings?
Victoria: Like, your shirt is so totally cool.
Brianna: It's from Paris.
Victoria: So are my earrings! EEEeeeee!
Brianna: EEEEeeee!

I was so glad to see Casey, I gave him a present.

Casey: What are these?
Me: A fossil and a piece of rose quartz.
Casey: I know, but —
Me (interrupting): I bought them at the Science Museum. Didn't you guess?
Casey: No.
Me: To replace the ones I lost.
Casey: You didn't have to —
Me: Yes, I did.
Casey: Well . . . thanks, Hayes.

* * *

We worked some more on our science project. Our igneous rocks had dried, so we
took two of them and made sedimentary
rocks.

Then we wrote a report on what we did.
Casey drew pictures of the blender and our
ingredients. I mounted the new report and
the old one on poster board. Casey tacked
up his new drawing and his old on another
piece of poster board.

It looked pretty good when we got finished. It looked like something that might
get us a good grade. It might even get us
extra credit.

Casey and I stood back to admire it.

Then I got my idea.

Chapter 14

Aeschylus wrote this in 458 B.C. All of his future is now past! Everyone has forgotten it.

My future is still ahead of me. And I <u>can't</u> forget it!

The science fair is tonight. Casey and I are going to set up our exhibit today in school. So will everyone else.

My whole family is coming to see the science fair.

Alex is excited because Casey will be there.

I am excited because the project is <u>finally</u> done!

And because I added a surprise to it. No one knows. I haven't told Casey. I haven't told my friends or family.

What will they think? What will Ms. Kantor think? What will Mrs. McMillan think? Will we get a good grade? Will we get extra credit? Will we get a prize?

My "surprise" isn't exactly scientific. It adds something to the project, though. And that's all the hint I'm going to give you, journal!

The Hayes family van pulled into a parking space behind the school. All around them, parents and students were getting out of cars.

"There's Natalie!" Abby cried. She rolled down the window and called to her friend.

Natalie was carrying a plate of cookies. "Hi, Abby!" she yelled.

Her father was right behind her. He turned to wave to Abby's parents.

Paul Hayes turned off the engine and opened the

car door. "There's quite a crowd here tonight," he commented.

"Don't forget you have to take me to the high school in twenty minutes," Eva reminded him. "I have a lacrosse game."

"And I have a Drama Club meeting," Isabel added.

Abby's mother sighed. "We're all so busy. I have a board meeting. But I still have plenty of time to see Abby's exhibit."

She gave her daughter a quick hug.

"I've already seen Abby's exhibit," Isabel grumbled. "I don't know why Eva and I have to come."

"You might be surprised!" Abby told her older sister. She picked up a grocery bag. Inside were two bottles of apple juice and some cups. Ms. Kantor had asked the students to bring refreshments.

"How?" Isabel asked. "Did you change the poster-board color?"

"You'll see," Abby said.

"We're a family," Olivia Hayes pointed out. She reached inside the car for her sweater. "It's important for us to support one another."

"There's Casey!" Alex cried. He sprinted down the sidewalk after him.

"Alex supports Casey," Eva said drily.

The rest of the Hayes family walked up to the school.

"Welcome to the Lancaster Elementary fifth-grade science fair." The principal, Ms. Yang, stood in the entranceway to greet the families and students.

"How's high school?" she asked Isabel and Eva.

"Not bad," the twins answered in unison. "Pretty good." They looked at each other and burst out laughing.

"It's a twin thing," Abby explained. Her sisters sometimes said the same thing at the same time.

"Did your older sisters help you with your science project?" Ms. Yang asked Abby.

"No, my younger brother did." She looked around for Alex, but he had disappeared. Casey was nowhere in sight, either.

The gym, where they had set up the exhibits, was packed. There were exploding volcanoes, animal mazes, levers and pulleys, and electrical circuits that lit up when you connected them correctly. There were parents and students and brothers and sisters. There were teachers and aunts and grandparents. Ms. Kantor rushed around with a camera, taking pictures of everyone.

"Hi!" Abby said to all her friends. "Hi!"

Her project was displayed on a table in the middle of the gym. Casey stood in front of it, explaining to parents and other students how he and Abby had made the rocks in a blender. Alex stood next to him, listening to every word.

"There you are, Hayes," Casey said. "I — "

"You missed it, Abby!" Alex interrupted. "The mayor was here! He looked at your project!"

"What was the mayor doing here?" Abby asked.

"He came to see me," Brianna bragged. "My cousin works for him."

At the table next to them, Brianna and Victoria had arranged half a dozen T-shirts. They had charts and graphs ranking each one. Each shirt was color-coded. On the graphs, each was represented by a different color gel pen.

"Our project is the coolest," Brianna bragged. "The mayor said we applied science to fashion."

Victoria looked annoyed. "My cousin who, like, owns a factory is coming, too. Doesn't your aunt work in his mail room?"

"Only because she wants to," Brianna said. "My aunt could get a job anywhere. She's the best."

"It must run in the family," Casey muttered.

"Someone has to do a scientific study of the 'B' gene," Abby whispered back.

"Abby!" Bethany waved to her from across the room. "Come say hello to Blondie!"

Abby threaded her way through the crowd. Bethany and Crystal's table was surrounded with curious onlookers. They were watching Blondie, Bethany's beloved hamster, scoot down the passageways in search of food.

"She's so intelligent," Bethany cooed.

Crystal bumped into the table. Their report fell on the floor. "Sorry!" she said.

"Good thing I brought extra tape," Bethany said.

"Sorry!" Crystal said as she dropped the report a second time.

Bethany rolled her eyes.

"Gotta go back," Abby told them. "Casey's all alone — except for Alex."

Casey hadn't said a word about the surprise yet. She wondered if he had noticed it.

"Hey, Hayes," Casey said. He was leafing through Abby's report on rocks. He put it down and smiled at her.

"Where's Alex?" Abby asked.

"He went off with Isabel. Your parents were just here. They'll be back. I — " he began.

"There's Ms. Bunder!" Abby cried. The creative writing teacher was dressed in black pants and a blue silk top. She wore sandals and had on a silver necklace.

Standing next to her was a tall bearded man in blue jeans and a T-shirt.

"Does Ms. Bunder have a boyfriend?" Abby wondered out loud. "She never said anything about him in class!"

Casey shrugged. His class didn't have creative writing with Ms. Bunder. "I wanted to — " he began again.

"I'll be right back!" Abby rushed off to say hello to her favorite teacher.

Ms. Bunder was talking to Zach's parents. She smiled at Abby, who waited for a break in the conversation. More parents approached.

"I'll catch you later," she said to Abby.

Disappointed, Abby headed back to her table. She wanted to tell Ms. Bunder about the surprise. Well, she'd show her later. Ms. Bunder would like it!

"*Finally*, Hayes!" Casey exclaimed. He looked grumpy. "You're leaving me all alone here!"

"Sorry," Abby said. "I *had* to say hi to Ms. Bunder."

"I just wanted — " Casey began.

"Jessica!" Abby cried. She waved wildly to her best friend. "I haven't seen your project! And I haven't seen Natalie's, either!"

"You haven't seen *ours*," Casey muttered.

"I won't be long — promise!" Abby said.

As she hurried toward Jessica's table, her mother emerged from the crowd.

"Abby!" she cried. "Your father and I have been looking for you."

"'I'm going to see Jessica's project," Abby said. "She studied the effects of pollution on viewing the night sky."

Her mother took her arm. "That sounds wonderful, but Eva, Isabel, and I have to leave soon," she said. "Let's go back to your table. I want you to show us *your* project."

The entire Hayes family had converged around the project table.

"You're back," Casey said in disbelief. "The posse must have rounded you up."

"It did," Abby said. "Sorry I — " She stopped in the middle of her sentence. Her mother was examining their homemade rocks.

"Casey and I made those in the blender, Mom."

Olivia Hayes looked startled. "I suppose your father said it was okay."

"I did," Paul Hayes said.

Abby's mother sighed. "I'll count my blessings. At least it wasn't our new food processor."

"These are great drawings of natural habitats," Isabel said to Casey.

"The report is good, too," Eva said.

"Casey and Abby did the *best* project!" Alex said proudly.

"Sshhhh!" Abby held a finger to her lips. "Don't let Brianna know!"

"Why not?" Eva said. "It's good to be competitive." She glanced at her watch. "Speaking of competitive, we have to leave soon. I don't want to be late for the game."

"Just a minute," Paul Hayes said. "I haven't finished looking at everything." He picked up another report. "What's this?" He turned the page. "'A Sizzling Scientific Surprise. A Tale of Two Projects,'" he read. "By Abby Hayes."

"Is this part of the science project?" Olivia Hayes asked her daughter.

"Well, uh, not really, but sort of — " Abby stopped. She was starting to sound like Victoria.

Isabel leaned over her father's shoulder. "Is this the surprise, Abby?"

"Uh, yeah, I guess so," Abby said, her face hot. She glanced at Casey. "I, uh, well — "

Paul Hayes handed the paper to his wife. "Read this," he said.

A Sizzling Scientific Surprise! A Tale of Two Projects!
by Abby Hayes

Something mysterious happened on the way to the science fair.

Abby Hayes and Casey Hoffman had assembled a rock collection from local and faraway sources. They had labeled their rocks and prepared detailed reports and drawings.

They had completed their work for the science fair — or so they thought.

✳   ✳   ✳

Then the entire rock collection disappeared one afternoon while Abby played soccer with Jessica and Sarah.

A search party was assembled. Members of the Hayes family scoured the park. They queried every person they met. They followed every lead.

No rock collection appeared.

Using scientific logic, Abby concluded that the collection was "lost, stolen, or strayed."

Its whereabouts remain a mystery, even today.

A period of scientific inquiry followed. Casey and Abby still had the report and drawings.

Using the scientific method, they examined their choices. Assemble another rock collection? Throw out everything and start anew? Or build on their work for a new science project?

They chose the third. It was the most logical. Casey found the perfect project. They made igneous rocks in the blender.

They wrote up a new report, but kept the old one, too.

Conclusion: Two projects can be better than one!

Abby and Casey learned about rocks.

They also learned about mistakes, discovery, and starting over again.

"Great job," Olivia Hayes said. "I'm so proud of you."

Paul Hayes gave his daughter a hug. "Terrific, honey."

"Is that all you have to say?" Abby asked, disappointed. Parents always said things like "great" and "terrific" and "proud."

"It's true!" her father insisted.

"Don't let failure stop you," Eva added. "That's how to have a winning team." She pointed to her watch again. "Dad, it's time to go!"

"Drama Club always starts late," Isabel said. "But I need to be there early. Good work, Abby."

"I helped a lot!" Alex said.

"Yes, you did," Casey agreed.

"You both did a wonderful job," Abby's parents said once more. "Abby, we'll pick you up in an hour."

The Hayes family left the gym.

Abby and Casey straightened out the exhibit.

"I want to tell you — " Casey began again, when Ms. Kantor and Mrs. McMillan appeared at their table.

Chapter 15

<u>Example:</u>
Ms. Kantor and Mrs. McMillan gave us an "A" on our rock project!

Hooray, Hooray! <u>Hooray!!!!</u>

Even though they did the same thing, it <u>wasn't</u> the same thing.
Ms. Kantor said: "I think these two deserve extra credit. Look, they did two projects and Abby wrote this wonderful 'Sizzling Scientific Surprise.'"

Mrs. McMillan said, "Abby wrote the 'Sizzling Scientific Surprise,' not Casey. That's what makes this project really special. Only Abby should get the extra credit."

Thinking fast, I said, "But Casey did just as much work as me. We divided it up. He did the drawings and experiments. I was the project writer."

Ms. Kantor smiled at me.

"That's very persuasive," Mrs. McMillan said. "When you put it that way, it makes sense."

"So you'll give us both extra credit?" I said.

Mrs. McMillan picked up the blender rocks. She glanced at Casey's drawings and my reports one more time. "Yes."

"I think they deserve it," Ms. Kantor said.

Casey and I high-fived each other.

"Hey, thanks, Hayes," Casey said after they left. "You stuck up for me."

"Better than being stuck-up," I joked.

We both glanced in Brianna and Victoria's direction. The teachers were talking to them.

Brianna was arguing with Ms. Kantor. "An A+ is the only mark I'll accept," she said.

"Like, we bought all these T-shirts and gel pens," Victoria said. "We deserve an A+ for the coolest project in the fifth grade. We spent more money than, like, anyone else."

"This is about science, not money," Ms. Kantor said.

"When you're a teacher, you can give yourself all the A+'s you want," Mrs. McMillan said. "For now, you're getting a B."

"B?" Victoria said.

"B!" Brianna shrieked.

Off the Mark
A play by Abby Hayes

Place: you know where
Time: you know when
Cast of Characters: you know who

Brianna: B is for best, isn't it?
Victoria (annoyed): Casey and Abby got,

like, an A for a bunch of rocks!

Brianna: They weren't even real rocks! Just a bunch of mushed-up paper!

Victoria: Like, our project was so much more _real_.

Enter Bethany with hamster in her arms.

Brianna: What did you get?

Bethany: B+! That's the best mark I've ever gotten in science. (Kisses hamster.) Thanks, Blondie!

Brianna (dramatically): B+???? Truth and justice are _dead_!

Bethany (holding hamster out to Brianna and Victoria): Want to pet her?

Victoria: Eeeuuu. Nasty. Get it away from me.

Bethany: You're hurting Blondie's feelings.

Victoria: Hamsters smell. Their eyes are, like, red.

Bethany: Blondie is listening!

Enter Natalie.

Natalie: We got an A on our project!! Hooray!

Brianna (sinks back onto a chair): They got an A. We got a B.

Victoria: Do you have to tell, like, every-one? Shut up, already!

The curtain falls. The play is over. So is the science fair.

I asked Casey if he liked my "Sizzling Scientific Surprise."

Casey said yes. (He had been trying to tell me all evening.)

"It tied together our two projects," he said. "It made them work together. It described how we worked together."

"I wish they had given out prizes!" I cried.

"We'd have gotten the Surprise Prize," Casey said.

Maybe Ms. Kantor will give it to us to-morrow? (It's never too late to give a Sur-prise Prize!) No, probably not.

Extra credit and an A are enough for now. . .

Casey and I wandered outside. The PTA was selling ice cream by the playground.

"Ice cream!" I cried.

Casey pulled some dollar bills out of his pocket. "I'll treat you. My mom said I should. She said it was nice of your parents to let us ruin your blender."

"We didn't ruin it. I washed it out right away," I said. "The container got stained blue, that's all. I don't think anyone will notice."

"Probably not," Casey said. "What kind of ice cream do you want?"

"Cherry chocolate chip. One scoop."

"Is that all, Hayes?" Casey asked. "Two scoops are better than one."

"If you say so, Hoffman," I replied.

One last word . . .

Wednesday still

"All's well that ends well."

— *William Shakespeare*

Riding into the Sunset Calendar

Ha, ha, ha, ha! Surprised you, didn't I? I bet you didn't expect a quote at the <u>end</u> of a journal entry!

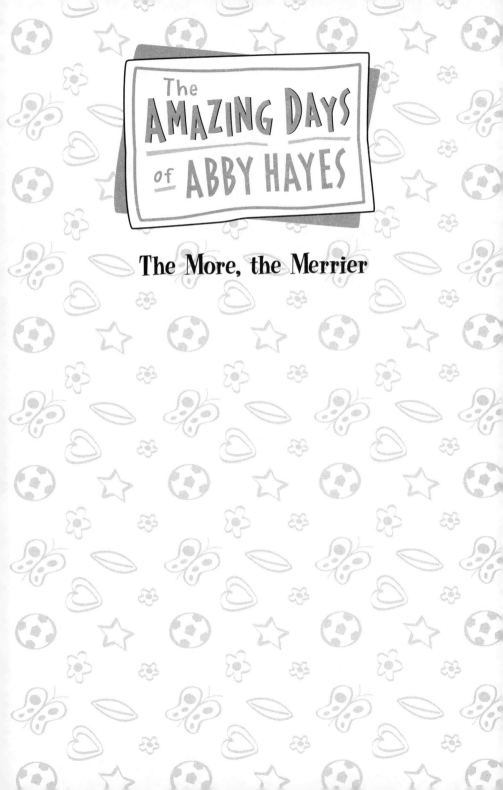

The
AMAZING DAYS
of ABBY HAYES

The More, the Merrier

To Miko

Chapter 1

Thursday

"The heart has its reasons . . ."

—Blaise Pascal

Funny Valentine Calendar

<u>Reasons my heart wants to have a</u> "Hooray! It's Summer!" party for the entire fifth grade:

1. It'll be fun.
2. All my friends will come.
3. We can celebrate the end of school.
4. We can eat watermelon, ice cream, hamburgers, hot dogs (or tofu dogs for Bethany), and potato salad.
5. The girls can compete against the boys (ha-ha-ha).
6. We can build a bonfire and make s'mores!

* * *

There is only one possible problem: Mom and Dad. Will they understand my reasons for having a party? Will they "listen to my heart"? (Ugh! That sounds like a medical checkup!)

Maybe they'll listen to my lungs or brain or kidneys. They'll all say the same thing. Every part of me wants to throw a party!!!!

What will Mom and Dad say? Will they let me have it? Isabel and Eva throw parties all the time. They are always popular!

I hope Mom and Dad will say yes!

"Guess what?" Abby whispered to her best friends, Jessica and Natalie, in class. Their teacher, Ms. Kantor, was collecting math homework. The three girls had just handed theirs in.

Natalie glanced up from the book she was reading under her desk. "What?"

"I'm going to ask my parents if they'll let me have an end-of-the-year party!" Abby announced.

"You think they'll say yes?" Jessica asked. She pushed a strand of long brown hair away from her face.

"Why not?" Abby said. "My older sisters have parties all the time."

"Lucky," Natalie said, shutting her book and slipping it into her desk. "My parents won't let me or my brother have parties."

"I have all my arguments prepared," Abby said. It helped having a mother who was a lawyer and an older sister who was a debating champ. In ten years of living with them, she had learned a thing or two.

"I hope they agree," Natalie said.

"I'm going to invite the entire fifth grade," Abby continued. "Ms. Kantor's class *and* Ms. McMillan's."

"Everyone?" Jessica asked with a frown. "Even Brianna?"

"It wouldn't be everyone without her," Abby said.

"Ugh," Jessica said.

The three girls glanced over to where Brianna sat, surrounded by a group of admirers. She wore a pale blue lace T-shirt over a short shiny silver skirt. She had on tiny earrings and colored lip gloss.

"My dance recital last night was the *best*," Brianna bragged loudly enough to be heard across the room. "Fifty-two people came to see me."

"I wonder if fifty-two people watched her eat breakfast," Natalie murmured. "She probably chews the best, too."

"If Brianna comes to your party, so will Victoria," Jessica warned Abby. "She's even worse."

"If that's possible," Natalie added.

Victoria was in Ms. McMillan's fifth-grade class. She and Brianna had become friends when they worked on a science fair project together. If Brianna was the best, Victoria was the coolest. She was also the meanest.

Abby shook her head. "No one will be left out," she insisted.

"They'll ruin the party," Jessica predicted.

"No, they won't!" Abby replied. "It'll be such a big crowd, no one will notice them."

"Ha," Natalie said.

Abby scowled at her friends. "If I don't invite them, they'll ruin my life!"

"You have a point," Jessica admitted.

"I wouldn't want Brianna mad at me," Natalie agreed.

Jessica bent over her notebook, then held it up for Abby and Natalie to see. She had doodled a picture of Brianna with a thick, scowling brow and a thundercloud over her head.

"Put a bolt of lightning in her hand," Abby advised Jessica.

Jessica smiled and picked up her pencil again. The three girls crowded around the drawing.

Ms. Kantor clapped her hands. "Back to your seats, everyone!"

Abby looked up. Ms. Bunder, her favorite teacher, had just come into the classroom.

Ms. Bunder came to Ms. Kantor's class once a week, to teach creative writing. She wore black slim-fitting pants and a silk tank top. Her necklace was silver and so were her earrings. Her eyes sparkled as she walked up to the blackboard and began to tape pictures on it.

"What are we doing today?" Mason demanded. He stuck a fat finger into his nose.

"*Eeeeeuuuuu*," Bethany squealed. "Yuk."

Jessica rolled her eyes. "He's *so* disgusting."

Ms. Kantor took a stack of papers and sat down at the back of the room. "Sssshhh!" she said to the class. "Quiet!"

Ms. Bunder taped the last picture to the blackboard and turned to face the fifth-graders. "We're going to write about our rooms," she announced.

"Yay!" Abby cheered. Ms. Bunder could ask her to write about the basement or the attic or the backyard shed. Abby loved writing about *anything*.

Ms. Bunder continued. "I want you to think about your room. What does it look like? Is it a special place? What do you do in your room? How do you feel when you're there?"

"Read!" Natalie said.

"Play cards and watch my hamster," Bethany said.

"Sleep," Tyler said.

"Write in my journal!" Abby cried.

"Is your room the way you want it?" Ms. Bunder asked. "How would you make it different? What kind of room would you like to have when you grow up?"

Brianna raised her hand. "I plan to live in a mansion. It'll have an indoor swimming pool and a movie room and . . ."

Mason burped loudly. "My room will be full of junk," he said.

"His mind already is," Abby murmured.

"Look at the rooms that I just taped on the

board," Ms. Bunder advised. "Maybe they'll inspire you to think about *your* room in a new way."

Abby studied the blackboard. "I don't like those girlie-girl rooms," she whispered to Natalie, pointing to a picture of a bedroom done up in pink, with a canopy bed and frilly curtains.

"Me, neither," Natalie whispered back. "I'd like to live in a chemistry lab. Or a castle."

Abby stared at a picture of a room painted in black-and-white zebra stripes. "Isn't that one great?"

"I hate it!" Jessica said. "It'd make me dizzy to live there."

"I'd want to draw in all the white spaces," Natalie said. "Or splash paint on them." She peered down at her white sneakers, which were covered with splotches of color. "Just like my sneakers."

"Okay, let's get started," Ms. Bunder said. "This is an assignment that you might like to complete at home. It's due next week."

"It's *home*work," Abby joked. "Get it?"

Her friends rolled their eyes.

"Casey would get it," Abby said.

"I thought you didn't like him," Natalie said.

Abby shrugged. "He's okay."

Casey was in the other fifth-grade class. He and

Abby had been science fair partners. At first they hadn't gotten along, but Abby had come to like him. He had the same sense of humor that she had.

"Are you inviting him to your party?" Jessica asked.

"Of course!" Abby exclaimed. "And Sarah, too."

Sarah had been Jessica's science fair partner. She and Jessica had become friends while working on a project about the stars and pollution.

"Good," Jessica said. For the first time since they had started talking about the party, she smiled at Abby.

Ms. Bunder walked over to Abby's desk. "Are you thinking about your room?" she asked.

"I'm thinking about my Hooray! It's Summer! party," Abby replied. "Maybe I'll have it in my room. Or maybe not." Forty or fifty kids wouldn't fit in her room. At least, not all at once.

"It sounds like fun," Ms. Bunder said with a smile. "Now start working on the assignment."

Abby picked up her purple pen and began to write down her thoughts about her room.

What were they, anyway?

My room: It has two windows, a door, and a closet. (Exciting.)

My room: It has a floor covered with a rug. There's a bedspread on the bed and curtains on the windows. (Wow.)

My room: I go to sleep there. (Snore.)

This is the most boring essay I have ever written, and I think I am going to stop writing now before I put myself to slee—

Abby dropped her pen with a clatter. Just a minute ago, she had been excited about this new assignment from Ms. Bunder. But now she didn't know what to write.

Wasn't her room special? Why wasn't there anything to say about it?

Chapter 2

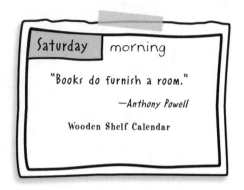

Saturday | morning

"Books do furnish a room."
—Anthony Powell

Wooden Shelf Calendar

So do calendars! In my room, I have only one bookcase, but walls of calendars.

<u>What I see when I look at my room</u>:
1. Calendars
2. Calendars
3. More calendars
4. And . . . you get the idea!

If I write about my room for Ms. Bunder's creative writing assignment, OF COURSE I have to write about my calendars! Why didn't I think of that in the *first place? Because I have been thinking about my party!*

Casey Hoffman dribbled the basketball down the Hayes driveway, passed it to Abby, and cheered as she made a basket.

"Your shots are getting better, Hayes," he said.

"Follow-through helps, Hoffman," Abby told him.

Casey nodded. He had dark hair, dark eyes, and ears that stuck out just a bit. Half an hour ago, he had rung Abby's doorbell and asked her to play basketball.

"Too bad Alex isn't here," Abby said. "He'll be mad that he missed you."

"Tell him we're playing baseball tonight in the park. He can join us." Casey tossed the ball through the hoop.

"Sure," Abby said, retrieving the ball. "He'll like that."

Abby's younger brother worshiped Casey. He followed him around and hung on his every word. As far as Abby was concerned, Casey was just *okay*; she liked him some of the time.

All right, she liked him *most* of the time. He wasn't annoying like Mason and Tyler and Zach. He wasn't giggly and hamster-crazy like Bethany. He wasn't better than she was at everything like her SuperSibs. He got most of her jokes. Even when her friends didn't think she was funny, Casey did.

"Did I tell you about my party?" she asked.

"Is it your birthday?" Casey frowned. "I'm not very good at figuring out presents."

"I want to have a Hooray! It's Summer! party," Abby explained. "I want to invite the entire fifth grade. We'll have it in my backyard. If my parents let me," she added.

"Great!" Casey said. "I hope they do." He threw the ball to Abby.

"Me, too," Abby said. "I'm asking them tonight." She took a deep breath. Her parents *had* to say yes.

"What are you planning?" Casey asked. "Movies? Volleyball? Charades?"

"We'll build a bonfire and make s'mores," Abby said. "We'll play games and talk."

"That sounds like fun," Casey began, when an all too familiar voice interrupted him.

"Abby and Casey. Together at last," Victoria cooed.

Victoria and Brianna stood at the edge of the driveway. The two best-dressed girls in the fifth grade both wore flowered capri pants, lace-edged T-shirts, colored bangles, and shiny lip gloss.

"They're a matching set," Abby said under her breath. Casey began to laugh.

"Casey and Abby," Brianna sighed. "The two of you just can't stay apart."

"The two of us just have to shoot hoops," Abby retorted. She tossed the ball back to Casey, who threw it into the basket.

"Hoops? You're, like, totally on a date," Victoria said.

"We're on a fig," Abby said.

"Dried or fresh?" Casey asked.

"*What* are they talking about?" Victoria asked Brianna.

Brianna shrugged. "Who knows?"

Victoria turned to Abby. "I, like, heard about your party."

"I haven't gotten permission yet," Abby warned.

"My parents let me have all the parties I want," Brianna boasted. "We have them catered."

"Is this an exclusive party?" Victoria asked. "Are you inviting only the coolest kids?"

"I'm inviting the entire fifth grade. It's a Hooray! It's Summer! party," Abby explained.

"You're inviting everyone?" Victoria asked. "Like, boys?"

Abby nodded her head.

"*Fifth*-grade boys?"

"Yes," Abby said. "Mason, Tyler, Zach, Jonathan, Casey . . ."

"Why don't you invite sixth-grade boys?" Victoria suggested. "They're, like, totally better."

"I invite sixth- and seventh-grade boys to *my* parties," Brianna bragged. "Are you having dancing? Or a band?"

"We're having games and a picnic," Abby said.

"Games?" Brianna said. "What kind?"

"Volleyball and races and kickball . . ."

Victoria wrinkled her nose. "That's so, like, elementary school."

"Hayes will throw a great party." Casey leaped to her defense. "Everyone will have a good time."

"Thanks, Hoffman," Abby said.

"Hayes? Hoffman?" Brianna repeated. "Are you two for real?"

"They're, like, *so* adorable," Victoria sneered.

"Will you both come to my party?" Abby asked, trying to change the subject. "I mean, if my parents say yes."

She hoped Brianna and Victoria would say no.

"Like, you know, if I'm not *totally* busy," Victoria said.

"Without us, your party won't be the same," Brianna added.

"It sure won't," Abby agreed.

Victoria checked her watch. "Brianna!" she squealed. "We have to get back to my house. My cousin is going to be there in, like, fifteen minutes."

Brianna sighed. "And leave Abby alone with her boyfriend?"

"He's *not* my boyfriend," Abby insisted.

"Sure, he isn't," Brianna smirked.

"Good-bye, lovebirds," Victoria said. "Come *on*, Brianna!" She grabbed Brianna by the arm and pulled her onto the sidewalk.

"Tweet, tweet!" Abby called.

As they disappeared down the street, Abby turned to Casey. "They're, like, *so* obnoxious!"

"Yep," Casey agreed. He picked up the basketball and tossed it to her.

Abby threw it hard. It bounced off the backboard. She threw the ball again and missed entirely.

"They're going to ruin my party if they come," she

said, frowning. "Jessica already said so. She's probably right."

"Maybe they won't even show up."

Abby brightened. "Really?"

"Your party is so, like, elementary school," Casey mimicked. "It's, like, totally for babies."

Abby passed him the ball. "I'll have a kindergarten party. We'll take naps, build blocks, and play Farmer in the Dell."

"That'll keep them away, Hayes." Casey swished the ball into the basket.

"And everyone else, too."

Casey grinned. "I don't think so. I bet lots of kids in my class will come."

"What can I do about Brianna and Victoria?" Abby asked.

"Don't worry about them," Casey said.

"Right," Abby agreed. She took the ball and shot it into the basket.

It *was* her party, not Brianna's or Victoria's! And it was going to be a great party! If her parents let her have it.

"When are you going to get permission?" Casey asked.

"Soon," Abby promised.

Chapter 3

"Hope for the best and
prepare for the worst."

Winter Storm Calendar

No! I will <u>only</u> hope for the best: a
party (DUH!) with everyone there. I will
<u>not</u> prepare for the worst: my parents' re-
fusal.

I won't even think about it. They
<u>CAN'T</u> say no! I'd rather have ten Bri-
annas and thirty Victorias attend my party
than have no party at all!

<u>The Great Party Debate</u>
Taking place in the Hayes living room.
Now! In living color!

* * *

The contestants:

1. Paul Hayes and Olivia Hayes, the parents of four children

2. Abby Hayes, the middle child

The odds are stacked against Abby Hayes. She must take on two adults—and one of them is a lawyer! But the brave ten-year-old will not let it stop her from arguing why she deserves to throw a party for the entire fifth grade.

The three contestants sit down together. Paul Hayes sips his coffee. Olivia Hayes squirts lotion on her palm and rubs it into her hands. Abby Hayes pulls at a hangnail.

After a few exciting moments like this, Abby boldly strikes the first blow.

"I want to throw a party for the entire fifth grade," she declares.

"_NO!_" the Hayes parents exclaim simultaneously.

Will the debate end right here? Will Abby run to her room in tears?

No. She is prepared! She has anticipated her parents' reaction and has worked out her arguments in advance.

Abby recites a list of the parties her twin ninth-grade SuperSisters have thrown in the last six months alone.

"Eva gave parties for the lacrosse team, the softball team, and the swim team. Isabel had parties for the debate team, the student council, the drama club, and the honor society."

Olivia Hayes is not impressed. "Those were small parties," she points out. "You want a large party."

"So???" Abby retorts.

This brilliant reply fails to impress her parents.

Abby unveils her next argument.

"Seven parties of approximately twenty people each equals one hundred and forty people, more or less, entertained at our house by my twin sisters." Abby rattles off the statistics. "That equals a SuperSib Super Bash three point five times bigger than the party I'm asking for!"

"Your math is improving," Paul Hayes comments. "However, seven small- to medium-sized parties can't be exchanged for one big one."

"Why <u>not</u>?" Abby demands.

"<u>Because,</u>" her parents reply.

Stunned by her parents' logic, Abby says nothing. For a moment, the debate appears to be at a standstill, with the Hayes parents winning.

Suddenly, in a surprise recovery, Abby jumps to her feet and marches up and down the living room.

"Fifth-graders have a right to parties as much as ninth-graders! Especially when there are two of them and only one of me!

"Eva and Isabel had seven separate parties this year! I had zero! Do you think this is fair? Or just? Or right?" she asks.

The Hayes parents sigh.

Olivia Hayes appeals to her middle daughter. "Are you sure you don't want a small party? Why don't you invite Jessica, Natalie, and Bethany for a sleepover?"

Abby Hayes holds firm. "I want a big party or nothing."

Paul Hayes frowns. Olivia Hayes appears to be thinking. (Or perhaps she's worrying about a court appearance tomorrow?) Abby Hayes crosses her fingers and recites all the magic words she knows.

Olivia Hayes speaks first. "I'd like to say no, but your arguments are irrefutable."

"Huh?" Abby says.

"That means no one can disagree with what you've just said," Paul Hayes explains.

"Okay. Sure. Whatever." Abby wonders why her parents are throwing new vocabulary words at her right now.

Her mother smiles.

"Irrefutable," Abby repeats, just in case this is the magic word that will make her parents say yes. "Will you let me have the party?"

Paul Hayes thinks about it. "It'll be a lot of work," he warns her. "Are you up for it?"

"Yes!" Abby cries.

"You'll be responsible for planning and invitations," Olivia Hayes adds. "And you'll have to clean up, too."

"Of course!!!" Abby promises. "I'll do anything to have a party with all my friends. I'll scrub floors, I'll wash windows, I'll even mow the lawn."

Paul and Olivia Hayes exchange glances. Abby holds her breath.

"Yes, you can," they (finally) say.

"Thank you! Thank you! Thank you!" Abby flings her arms around both parents and kisses them. "You're the best parents who ever lived!"

VICTORY!

Hooray! Hooray! Hooray! Was it really that easy? They didn't make me promise to do thirty years of hard labor or even one weekend of sweeping out the garage or basement. (Ha-ha-ha.) All I have to do is plan, send out invitations, and clean up. A piece of cake! Speaking of cake, I better think about what kind I want.

Chocolate? Or vanilla? Or carrot cake? Or orange or lemon cake? And what kind of decorations should it have?

I also have to come up with a menu. And decide on games. And design the invitations.

I have a lot of decisions to make! And the party is only a few weeks away!

Chapter 4

I agree! Why don't they sell six-foot pencils in stationery stores??? Or charcoal sticks as big as stilts? Or telescoping paintbrushes?

<u>What I would draw on my ceiling (if I could)</u>:
1. My friends
2. Myself (wearing earrings!)
3. My kitten, T-Jeff
4. Purple swirls

* * *

<u>What I wouldn't draw or write on my ceiling</u>:

1. My journal entries
2. My party invitations
3. My essay for creative writing

I have to finish my creative writing essay before I print out party invitations. I wish my parents didn't keep track of my homework!

I have only written one paragraph so far. It's about my calendars (of course). I wonder what my friends are writing about <u>their</u> rooms?

Abby closed her journal and lay back on her bed. For a moment, she stared at the blank ceiling. She imagined it covered with purple swirls, like tinted clouds. She'd love to wake up to a purple, billowy ceiling.

"A purple, billowy ceiling," she said out loud. She reached for the draft of her essay and wrote the words down one side of the paper.

She reread the paragraph she had already written.

In my room, I'm surrounded by time. My calendars are like trees that drop their leaves every thirty days. Every month I have new scenery on my walls.

That was fine — but she had nothing else, except "purple billowy ceiling." Ms. Bunder wouldn't accept it, and neither would her parents!

Abby sat up. She began to write again.

If I didn't have my calendars, my room would be a plain, ordinary room. No one would know anything about me.

No one would know that I have a cat. T-Jeff's food dish and water bowl and kitty litter are in Isabel's room.

No one would know that I love to write. I keep my purple journal hidden where my spying SuperSisters can't find it and read it.

No one would know that I love purple, either! I have only a few purple things:

1. My journal
2. My pen
3. A bear that Grandma Emma gave me

4. Some barrettes and hair clips

5. A small plastic fortune-telling ball

I wish I had a purple billowy ceiling! I wish I had a purple rug and purple curtains! I wish I could turn my room into a Palace of Purple!

Abby put down her pen. She picked up the paper and went to find her parents.

"Abby! Do you know where my tennis racket is?" Eva asked. She was dressed in shorts and a T-shirt. Her hair was pulled back into a ponytail. "I've been looking all over for it!"

"I haven't seen it," Abby said. "Do you know where Mom and Dad are?"

Eva shrugged. "Try the backyard."

Abby ran downstairs. Behind her, Eva yelled for her twin. "*Isabel!* Where's my tennis racket?"

In the backyard, her father was digging a vegetable plot. Her mother was pruning rosebushes.

"I finished my creative writing essay!" Abby announced, waving the draft in her father's direction. He was the one who usually checked her schoolwork. "All my other homework is done. May I print out the party invitations now?"

Paul Hayes put down the shovel. "Let's see what you've written," he said.

"It's the rough draft," Abby explained, handing him the paper. "I'll copy it over tomorrow."

Her father frowned as he read the essay. "It's a little short," he commented. "Especially for you."

"I don't have much to say about my room!" Abby answered. "Unless I quoted from all the calendars. Ms. Bunder would rather have me use my own words."

"She has a point," her father said. He looked at the essay again. "This seems fine."

"Hooray!" Abby cried. "May I use your computer?"

"Did you empty the dishwasher?" her mother called.

"Yes, Mom! I've done *all* my work!"

Her mother nodded. Her father handed back the essay. "I'll set you up on the computer as soon as I wash my hands."

"I can do it, Dad. I know what to do."

"Okay," her father said. "Just remember to exit when you're done."

"I *know*, Dad!" Abby began. She was about to tell him how well she understood the computer and its programs when Eva and Isabel appeared on the back porch.

Eva looked furious. So did Isabel.

"Mom! Dad! Isabel used my tennis racket!" Eva cried. "Without permission!"

"Eva! You said — " Isabel began. Her long dark hair was pulled back with a pink-and-silver barrette. She pulled impatiently on a stray lock as she faced her twin.

"I *didn't*!" Eva insisted.

"You did!" Isabel said. "Why are you bothering Mom and Dad with this?" she added primly. "Can't we work it out on our own?"

"NO!" Eva said.

Olivia Hayes put down her pruning shears. "Don't you have your own tennis racket, Isabel?"

"I did, but — "

"She lent it!" Eva finished her twin's sentence.

"And then Eva said — "

"I said nothing! I never gave you permission to use mine!"

"Not true!" Isabel retorted.

"Is too!" Eva shot back.

Abby glanced at her father. He had picked up his shovel and was breaking up a clod of dirt.

"Thief!" Eva cried.

"Liar!" Isabel accused.

Their mother interrupted. "You can use *my* tennis racket whenever you want, Isabel. Leave your sister's alone. End of argument."

The twins frowned at each other one last time. Then Eva ran back into the house, slamming the door behind her.

Isabel followed, with a second slam of the door.

"Another day, another argument," Paul Hayes said. "When will it end?"

"I'm going on the computer to print out the party invitations," Abby said. She hoped her sisters didn't plan on using it, too. She didn't want to tangle with either of them right now.

"There's rainbow-colored paper in my study," her mother said. "Take as much as you need."

"Great!" Abby said. She ran up the back porch stairs and opened the kitchen door.

Isabel and Eva were sitting at the kitchen table, drinking apple juice and chatting as if nothing had happened.

"Uh, hi," Abby said nervously. Her sisters were like two bombs that might explode at any moment. Or not.

"We're talking about your party, Abby," Eva said.

"You are?"

"How did you get Mom and Dad to agree to it?" Isabel studied her younger sister. "They never let *us* invite the entire fifth grade!"

"We're impressed," Eva continued. "We want to know your technique."

Abby poured herself a glass of juice. "Irrefutable logic," she said.

"*What?*" Eva asked.

"She out-argued them, dummy," Isabel informed her.

"Dummy?" Eva repeated. She glared at her twin.

"Never mind, silly," Isabel said. "What kinds of arguments did you use, Abby?"

Should she tell Isabel and Eva that she used *them* to get permission? Probably not. Abby drank her juice in one gulp and set the empty glass on the counter.

"Mathematical arguments," Abby replied. She took a step toward the kitchen door. "I have to go print out the invitations now."

Upstairs in her father's office, Abby turned on the computer monitor. She opened the program to make greeting cards.

First she flipped through illustrations. Did she want balloons? Or soccer balls? Or flowers? Or cakes? Or trees and ponds? Or teddy bears?

And what kind of type did she want?

Calligraphy? Plain? Gothic? Italic? Script? Block letters?

There were so many decisions to make!

Abby typed out the words "Hooray! It's Summer!" and tried them out in different fonts.

She added illustrations and took them away.

She experimented with textured backgrounds and plain ones.

Using her mother's rainbow paper, she printed out several trial invitations. None of them was quite right.

"Are you *still* here?" Isabel asked.

"I thought you'd be done hours ago," Eva added.

Abby glanced at the clock. Two hours had passed. It seemed like only a few minutes.

"They're almost done," she lied. "Just a few more minutes."

Isabel picked up one of the invitations. "You need help," she said.

Eva peered over her shoulder. "Why don't you make the type smaller and the background brighter?"

"I think the type should be larger," Isabel disagreed.

Abby snatched the invitation from her older sisters. "It's mine," she said. "I'll do it the way I want."

Isabel shrugged. "If that's how you feel."

"The illustrations are crooked," Eva said.

Abby frowned. "I don't want any help."

"Why not?" Isabel asked. "We've got experience and knowledge."

Eva slung her arm around her twin. "Yeah, we've got Twin Power."

"No!" Abby said.

Her sisters didn't listen. They grabbed another invitation from the printer and began to criticize it.

Chapter 5

Thursday

"The more, the merrier."

Lemming Calendar

The more <u>what</u>, the merrier?

1. The more kids at my party, the merrier.

2. The more calendars on my walls, the merrier.

3. The more sisters helping print out my invitations, the

. . . gloomier? . . . harder? . . . longer? . . . stupider?

None of these words sums up what happened when Eva and Isabel insisted on improving my invitations.

They argued for half an hour over

whether it should be Hooray! It's Summer!
or Hooray for Summer!

They argued whether I should print
swimming pools in the background or tennis
rackets.

They argued whether I should print all
the invitations on purple paper or rainbow
paper or plain white with colored designs.

They argued. . . .

AAAAAAARRRRRRGGGGGGGGHHHHH!

Twin Power?? No, Twin Powder Keg!

If Isabel and Eva hadn't been "helping"
me, I would have finished the invitations
on Tuesday night.

Instead, I had to finish printing them
out on Wednesday night, when my sisters
were out of the house. I hurried through
my homework and quickly copied my creative
writing essay.

(I didn't do as good a job on my writing as usual. I hope Ms. Bunder will understand!)

Now that they're finally done, the invitations look great!!! They are printed on Mom's rainbow-colored paper in a calligraphy font that Isabel suggested. There are balloons and stars in the background.

Eva told me to put the invitations in a plastic bag to protect them. (My sisters did have a few good ideas!)

The invitations are in my backpack, waiting to be passed out at recess, after class with Ms. Bunder. I can't wait!!!!!

In front of the class, Bethany held up a lovingly drawn picture of her hamster, Blondie, in her cage. "My room," she began. "My room is a deluxe hamster suite. My room is Blondie-centered. My room is hamster heaven."

The class listened attentively.

"We're going to take a tour of the rooms of the fifth grade," Ms. Bunder had said at the beginning of class. "We'll visit everyone's room — even if we never visit their house!"

Everyone cheered. Except Abby. She stared down at her desk.

It was one thing to hand in an assignment she'd written in a hurry. It was another to read it out loud. If she had known, she never would have rushed. She would have taken more time. She would have given it more thought. There must have been something else to say about her room.

Bethany concluded her essay with a description of a poster of Brianna hanging from her wall. "Yay, Brianna," Bethany said.

"You forgot to mention that it's a *signed* poster," Brianna corrected her.

As Bethany slid back into her seat, Natalie jumped up. "Can I go next, Ms. Bunder?" she cried.

Ms. Bunder nodded.

Natalie hurried to the front of the class. Her short dark hair was tousled and unruly. She began reading from a wrinkled, folded paper.

"My room is a Harry Potter shrine," she began. "I have Harry Potter sheets, curtains, clock, slippers, and bathrobe. I have read each of the Harry Potter books ninety-two times. I also have an international Harry Potter shelf, with books in seven different languages: Japanese, French, German, Spanish, Danish, Arabic, and Chinese. No, I can't read them, but maybe I will someday.

"Aside from that, I have a table with chemistry equipment and a bookcase filled with mystery and fantasy novels. I have a closet full of capes, swords, gowns, and unusual hats. And a hamster named Madame Curie."

"What an exciting room!" Ms. Bunder said.

The fifth-graders applauded. Abby sighed. Natalie's room sounded so — *Natalie*!

Mason lumbered to the front of the class. "My room is a disaster zone," he began.

The class laughed.

"My room looks like a hurricane hit it. There are clothes piled three feet high on the bed." Mason grinned at the class. "It's decorated with old pizza boxes, a broken lamp shade, and a cracked window. There's a DANGER sign on the door. If you walk in, you may not come out. Enter if you dare!"

"That was a very good description!" Ms. Bunder said. "But I hope you stretched the truth!"

"I stretched it like Silly Putty!" Mason said. He high-fived Zach on the way back to his seat.

"Next?" Ms. Bunder said. "Any volunteers? Brianna?"

"My essay is called 'Beauty and the Best,' " Brianna announced. She paused to flip her hair over her shoulder and to smile professionally at the class.

"My room is a reflection of me. It is the best room I have ever seen. I have my own audiovisual center, a large-screen television, a DVD player, a private phone line, a computer, and a canopy bed decorated with Belgian lace."

"It's 'Beauty and the Boast,' " Natalie whispered to Abby.

"Yes!" Abby agreed.

There was polite applause from the class and a "Yay, Brianna" from Bethany when Brianna finished her essay.

"That's quite a room, Brianna," Ms. Bunder said. She scanned the class. "Who hasn't read their essay?"

Abby squirmed in her seat.

"You're awfully quiet today, Abby," Ms. Bunder said. "Why don't you read next?"

Abby slowly made her way to the front of the room, unfolded her paper, and began to read.

"In my room, I'm surrounded by time. My calendars are like trees that drop their leaves every thirty days. Every month I have new scenery on my walls."

Her face was burning. No one else in the class had written anything like this. Would they laugh at her? Or just not get it?

She rushed through the rest of the essay, concluding, "I wish I could turn my room into a Palace of Purple!"

Abby glanced at her teacher and slunk back to her seat.

"Very interesting, Abby," Ms. Bunder said.

"Interesting," Abby repeated to herself. That was a word that everyone said. It meant nothing. It probably meant less than nothing.

"I liked it," Natalie whispered.

Abby grimaced. Natalie was her friend. Of course she liked it!

No matter what anyone said, Abby knew that her essay was one of the least exciting in the class. Not because she couldn't write — but because there was nothing to write about!

Her room wasn't a Harry Potter shrine, a disaster zone, or a hamster-lover's paradise. It wasn't a tree house — except in her imagination — or a palace of purple. It didn't reflect her personality or her tastes. It didn't have anything to do with Abby Hayes.

Her room was plain and ordinary, with a bunch of calendars stuck on the walls.

Chapter 6

I am <u>not</u> at ease in my room! Especially after hearing my classmates' essays!

Does this mean that I'm going to have a misfortune? (*Noooo!!!!*)

Does this mean that my party will be a disaster? (Help!!!!!)

Does this mean that my classmates will ask to see my room during the party? (*Noooo!!!!!* Help!!! That would be a misfortune AND a disaster!)

* * *

What My Classmates Will Probably Do
When They See My Room:
1. Laugh
2. Yawn
3. Run for the door

Maybe I should put a "Danger"
sign on the door. Or orange police
tape.
What I need is a "Danger!
Boring Room!" sign.

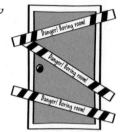

(Good thing I have my party to think
about!)

"Party invitations!" Abby called. She stood in the middle of the playground and held up a folded stack of colorful cards. "Come and get them!"

"Where's mine?" Mason demanded. "I'm a party animal!"

"I know that," Abby said, handing him a lime green invitation.

"Cool!" Tyler said, reading over Mason's shoulder. "A party for the whole fifth grade!"

Abby gave him an invitation. "I'm planning it myself."

"Make sure there's plenty of food," Zach advised her.

"Especially if you're inviting boys," Rachel added.

"Girls eat just as much as boys!" Megan protested.

"Yeah!" Mason burped in agreement.

"Eeeuuu! Disgusting!" Rachel said.

One by one, Abby distributed the invitations to her classmates. Then she went to find Jessica.

Jessica was upside down on the rings next to Sarah, who hung by her hands. Jessica swung by her knees. Her long brown hair trailed along the ground.

"Got party invitations?" Abby asked. She waved them in front of the two girls.

Jessica pulled herself up and dropped to the ground. "I can't believe your parents said yes!"

Abby nodded. "I'm planning the whole party by myself. They said I could do anything within reason."

"What about without?" Jessica teased.

"All my plans have a reason!" Abby said. "To have a good time!"

Sarah somersaulted over the rings and landed on her feet. Her face was red and perspiring.

"I hope you can come to my party," Abby said, giving her an invitation. She didn't know Sarah very well. Once or twice they had played soccer together. She was Jessica's friend, not hers.

Sarah pushed back a lock of damp hair from her forehead. She glanced at the invitation and stuffed it in her shorts pocket. Then she jumped back onto the rings and swung back and forth.

"Can you can get all the way across without falling?" Jessica challenged her.

"I can!" Sarah leaped for the next ring.

The two girls seemed to have forgotten about Abby.

"See you," Abby said. She hurried across the playground to look for Bethany and Natalie.

They were deep in conversation next to the slide.

"Hamsters are nocturnal," Bethany was saying. "They sleep during the day and play all night."

"I noticed," Natalie said, yawning.

"Party! Party! Party!" Abby interrupted them.

"Oh, great," Natalie said.

"Fun!" Bethany said. "I can't wait!"

Brianna came up behind them. Abby turned to give her an invitation.

"Colored xerox paper?" Brianna said, wrinkling her nose. "My party invitations are custom-printed on handmade paper with calligraphic lettering."

"I remember those," Bethany said.

"Oh, hello there," Brianna said, acknowledging her best friend with a wave of her hand. *"Comment ça va?"*

"Ssssuh *what?*" Natalie asked.

"It's French," Brianna informed her. *"Je parle le français."*

"Iay eferpray igpay atinlay," Natalie retorted. "I prefer pig latin."

"How about guinea pig latin?" Abby grinned at Bethany.

"Is there such a thing as hamster latin?" Bethany asked hopefully.

Brianna rolled her eyes. "Do you have any other topic of conversation besides hamsters?" she demanded.

"Like, I don't think so," Victoria said nastily as she joined the group of girls.

"Victoria!" Brianna squealed, turning her back on Bethany.

"Brianna!" Victoria squealed back. "I have the coolest new CD to play for you. It's by Tiffany Crystal."

"Oooooh!" Brianna shrieked. "I love her! She's the greatest!"

"The Tiffany Crystal concert is, like, soon," Victoria said. "Are you going?"

"I have free tickets," Brianna announced. "My cousin knows the electrician on Tiffany's tour."

"We're going together," Bethany said. "Aren't we, Brianna?"

Brianna didn't reply. She ignored her best friend. Instead, she linked arms with Victoria. The two girls began to sing one of Tiffany's platinum hits.

"Nasty sugar sweet," they blared.

Bethany looked depressed.

"Have an invitation to my party," Abby said. She thrust one into Victoria's hand.

"Wow, this is, like, so exciting," Victoria said sarcastically. "I can hardly wait."

Abby straightened up. "I'm having live music, a tent, and prizes!" she said. "My party is going to be *great*!"

"Esyay," Natalie agreed in pig latin.

"I'm glad your party isn't on the same day as the Tiffany Crystal concert," Bethany said. "Brianna and I love Tiffany."

Brianna turned to Victoria. "Have you seen my new lip gloss collection?"

"It's the best," Bethany said eagerly. "Brianna has the biggest lip gloss collection in the fifth grade."

"Come on, Brianna, let's go," Victoria said, making a face. "We can't talk here. Hamster ears are listening."

Without saying good-bye, the two girls walked away. Bethany trailed behind them for a few moments, then veered off toward a bench.

Natalie and Abby went over to join her.

"I hate Tiffany Crystal," Natalie said, sitting down next to Bethany. "She can't sing."

"She's okay," Bethany mumbled. "I just hope Brianna doesn't invite Victoria to the concert with us."

"Like, why not?" Abby mimicked. "Victoria is so, like, totally *sweet*!"

Bethany tried to smile.

Abby slung her arm around Bethany's shoulder. "Cheer up, Bethany. You're *so* much nicer than Victoria!"

"Yeah," Natalie agreed.

Bethany frowned. "Do you think Brianna knows that?"

Natalie and Abby looked at each other. They didn't say anything.

Abby got up to give out the rest of the invitations. She found Casey and asked him to hand out some to his classmates. When she returned, Bethany and Natalie were talking about hamsters again.

"Can we talk about another animal for a change?" Abby joked. "Like emus, ocelots, or mongooses?"

"Are you really having live music, a tent, and prizes at your party?" Natalie asked Abby.

"Well — "

"Don't worry, Abby. Your party will be *almost* as good as Brianna's," Bethany reassured her.

"Thanks, Bethany." Abby frowned. "I wish I hadn't promised all those things!"

She scuffed her foot in the dirt. "The live music is going to be a boom box," Abby said slowly. "The tent will be Alex's Cub Scout tent, and the prizes will probably be a bunch of pencils!"

"It still sounds like fun," Natalie said.

Abby just hoped that Brianna and Victoria wouldn't make fun of her party. They had a way of getting lots of kids on their side.

She also hoped that they wouldn't ask to see her room! Or go up there before she knew what they were doing.

She especially hoped that they wouldn't be too mean to Bethany.

Could someone put them in solitary confinement on the day of her party?

Chapter 7

Friday evening

"What is the hardest task in the world? To think!"

—Ralph Waldo Emerson

Impossible Dreams Calendar

7:15 p.m. I am trying to think about my room.

What does my room need? What can I do to make it better? Think! Think! Think!

What is in my room (aside from calendars):
1. A lamp (with peeling, ugly paint)
2. A bureau (with clothes spilling out of its drawers)
3. A bed (not made)

4. A chair (only one leg dented)
5. A mirror (smeared with fingerprints)
6. A clock (six minutes fast)
7. A desk (piled with papers and books)

Is there a 911 Room? My room needs first aid! It needs emergency care! Is there a room doctor in the house?

I want a room that I can show off to my friends and classmates!

I want a room that everyone will talk about!

I want a room that I will love spending time in!

I want an Abby room instead of an Anyone room.

<u>What I'd like in my room (aside from calendars)</u>:
1. A petting zoo
2. A water slide and a roller coaster

3. A basketball court
4. An earring store
5. My own computer
6. A bubble gum machine

Sure. Right. Yeah.

<u>What I could actually do to my room</u>
(aside from buying more calendars):
1. Make the bed
2. Vacuum the floor
3. Clear off the desk

Uh. Duh. Boring!!!
   If I clean my room now, I'll have to
clean it again before the party. (Why waste
energy? Once is enough!)

<u>Other ideas</u>:

Okay, never mind.

7:42 p.m.

Minutes I have been thinking: 27

Number of useful ideas I have had: 0

Will put self in <u>Hayes Book of World Records</u> for "Fiercest Brain Activity with Fewest Results."

Thinking <u>is</u> the hardest task in the world!

I must improve my room. I must improve my room. I must improve my room. I must . . . Okay, okay, I get the idea!

Mom says, "When you have a problem, think outside the box."

 What box is she talking about? A box of candy? A box of clothes? An empty cardboard box?
　　　My room looks like a box! (A messy, dull, boring one.) Maybe I'll go outside it to think outside it??!

7:48 p.m. Thinking Outside the Box.
1. Backyard. Dark and rainy. I thought

about umbrellas and raincoats and flash-lights. Ideas for room: Decorate with boots, raincoats, and umbrellas on wall? Flashlight theme?

2. Hallway. Tripped on Alex's Rollerblade. Stared at stain on the wall. Listened to shower running. Ideas for room: Install Rollerblading rink? Put in room-sized waterfall?

3. Living room. Sat on couch and watched TV. Ideas for room: Move into living room and forget about room altogether.

8:30 p.m. I can't think outside the box!!! Or inside it, either!

8:38 p.m. Went back upstairs. Passed Isabel's room. She was doing her nails (again). Was too dejected to ask Isabel how many times she had changed her nail color today. (She has broken all the world records in the <u>Hayes Book of World Records</u> for nail polish use.)

Isabel looked up. "Abby! I want to show you something!"

"What?"

"Come here!"

"Do I have to?"

"Yes!"

"Why?"

"Just come in my room!"

8:39 p.m. Went into Isabel's room. She was sitting at her desk with two trillion bottles of nail polish in front of her.

"That stuff stinks!" I said.

Isabel blew on her nails. "So? I like it."

"It rots your brain."

"Sure it does."

My sister didn't have to defend her beloved nail polish any further. She is the top student in the ninth grade.

"Uh, yeah, right," I mumbled.

"Look, Abby!" Isabel said. She held up her hands and waved them around in the air.

"Huh?"

"My nails, dummy!"

I stared at her nails. They were shiny, wet, and long. They were perfectly mani-cured. They were oval in shape. They were attached to her fingers. They were—

"Purple!!!!!" I yelled.

"I was wondering when you'd notice."

"They're great," I said.

She held out the bottle of nail polish. "I know you love purple. Do you want purple nails, too?"

"Thanks, Isabel!" I started to open the bottle.

"Take it to your room," Isabel said, pointing to a stack of books on her bed. "I have to study."

8:58 p.m. Went back to room with Isabel's purple nail polish. Painted nails deep, rich, glori-ous purple. Decided to wear purple shirt, purple barrettes, and purple socks the next day to coordinate.

9:07 p.m. Admired purple fingernails (and purple-spotted fingertips).

9:08 p.m. Looked around my room, then glanced down at purple fingernails.

9:09 p.m. Started to get an idea.

9:10 p.m. Looked around room. Looked down at nails. Looked around room again. Looked down at nails. Looked around room. Looked down at nails.

Kept doing this until I got dizzy.

9:13 p.m. <u>EUREKA!!!!!!!!!!!! I have my idea!!!!!!!</u>

9:13½ p.m. Jumped up from chair and leaped around room.

9:15 p.m. Ran into Isabel's room to give her a hug.

9:16 p.m. Ignored Isabel's baffled look. Ran back to room.

9:18 p.m. Admired nails. Looked around room one more time.

9:21 p.m. Counted money in drawer.

9:22 p.m. Put money in pocket of pants I plan to wear tomorrow.

9:26 p.m. Brushed teeth, put on purple pajamas, and climbed into bed.

Sweet dreams!

Chapter 8

Saturday morning

"Inspiration comes from
unexpected places."

—Ms. Bunder

Fifth-grade Creative Writing Class

Ms. Bunder is right!

I didn't get my inspiration from inside or outside of a box. It didn't come from thinking. It didn't come from watching television or from standing in the rain in the dark. It came from Isabel's fingernail polish.

(Does Isabel know that her fingernail polish is inspiring? Does she know that big ideas can come from a small bottle?)

Today I am going to buy a can of paint and a paintbrush. Today I am going to paint my lamp purple!!!!

* * *

Other plans:

Buy purple bedspread. (If Mom agrees!)

Find purple lamp shade. (Is there such a thing?)

Display purple toys on shelves. (Must start collection!)

My room will be a Palace of Purple! I will turn it into an awesome, amazing, astonishing, adorable, absolutely Abby abode!

"May I paint my lamp?" Abby asked her mother and father Saturday morning.

Her father raised his eyebrows. "Why not?" he said. "Or rather — why?"

"The last time we painted that lamp was when Isabel and Eva were babies," her mother reminded him. "It was in their nursery."

"The paint is peeling off," Abby said. "It's an ugly yellow."

"Ah," her father said, drinking the rest of his coffee.

"May I paint it?" Abby repeated. "It'll spruce up my room."

"Yes, but only with the windows open!" her father

said. "And lots of newspapers on the floor."

"Newspapers aren't good enough. She should put a drop cloth down," her mother advised. "Or even better, paint it outside."

Abby pointed to the window. "It's raining today. I have to do it in my room."

"We have leftover paint in the garage," her father said. "Odds and ends of blue, green, and yellow. You'll find enough to do a lamp base."

"But I want to paint it purple!" Abby cried.

"Purple?" her father said.

"Purple," Abby said firmly. "It's my favorite color. I want purple in my room."

Her mother nodded as if she understood.

"Do you think I can get purple sheets?" Abby asked her. "Or a purple bedspread?"

"Your bedspread is in good condition," her mother said. "And we have so many sheets. I don't want to buy any more."

Abby's face fell.

"But I'll buy purple cloth and make you new curtains," her mother promised.

"Yay!" Abby said. "Purple curtains!" She flung out her arms. "Mom! You're the greatest! There'll be purple everywhere!"

Her mother shook her head and then smiled.

"I'm going to the hardware store in an hour," her father said. "Will you be ready?"

"Yes!" Abby said.

Abby wandered through aisles of saws, hammers and drills, caulk and sealants, nails and screws, tape measures and plumbing snakes.

"I never knew there were so many tools in the world," she said to her father.

"The paint is over there," her father said. He pointed to a counter stacked high with paint cans. "Pick up some color cards, and find the perfect purple. Then ask for a pint of semigloss paint."

"A pint of semigloss paint," Abby repeated.

"You might even want a high gloss," he said. "Depends on how shiny you'd like it."

Abby looked at her purple fingernails. "About as shiny as these," she said.

"It's your room," her father said.

"Bright purple will perk it up," Abby told him.

"If you say so." He pointed to the other side of the store. "I'll be there if you need me. I've got a dozen things to buy."

"Okay. Thanks, Dad!" Abby said.

She headed over to the paint section.

"Where are the color cards?" she asked the woman behind the counter.

"Over there," she said.

"Do you have lots of purples?" she asked.

"Oh, yes!" the woman said.

She was right. There were rows of color cards with every shade imaginable. Abby pulled out six and compared the color chips to her fingernails.

"Do you need any help?" The woman followed her to the color card display. "I can show you what we have. Or you can browse on your own."

"I'm trying to find this color purple," Abby said, pointing to her nail polish.

"We've never had anyone match paint to nail polish before," the woman commented. She took the color cards from Abby and quickly looked through them.

"This one," she said. "Or this. It depends whether you like a redder purple or a bluer one."

"I like this one," Abby said. She read its name out loud. "The People's Purple."

"That's a strange color name," the woman said. "Sometimes I wonder who thinks up all those names."

"I'd call it Jumping for Joy," Abby said. That was how the color made her feel.

"That's a better one," the woman said. "Maybe you should go to work for the paint company."

Abby smiled. "I could think of hundreds of names for purple!" she cried. "Jumping for Joy, Particularly Purple, Great Grape, Purple Majesty . . ."

The woman led her to the cash register. "How much People's Purple do you need?" she asked. "And do you want flat, semigloss, or gloss?"

"I'm painting a lamp," Abby told her. "I might paint my desk and bureau, too."

"I'd take a gallon of either semigloss or gloss," the woman advised. "We have a sale right now, and you can get two gallons for the price of one."

"I'll take a gallon of the gloss," Abby said. "I mean, two."

With two gallons for the price of one, she'd have the People's Purple on hand for any purple project she could dream of. She could paint her chair, her bookcase, or her bed. Wait until her friends saw! They would be so impressed with her room!

"That'll be twenty-one ninety-five," the woman said. She hauled two gallons of the People's Purple onto the counter. "Here's a mixing stick, too. Do you need paintbrushes or rollers or drop cloths?"

"We have them at home," Abby said. She counted out the dollar bills in her pocket.

Her father came up next to her at the counter.

"I'll pay for that," he said.

"You will? Thanks, Dad!"

"Where's that pint of paint?" he asked, pulling out his wallet.

"I got two gallons." Abby pointed to the cans on the counter.

"Two *gallons*?" her father cried. "You don't need that much!"

"It's on sale, Dad!"

"No, Abby."

"But Dad," Abby protested, "I need at least a gallon. I might paint my desk and chair!"

"It's a two-for-one special," the woman explained. "You might as well take the extra gallon. It's free."

Her father shook his head. "We don't need two gallons of the People's Purple!"

"What if I decide to paint the old wicker chairs in the backyard?" Abby asked. "I might want purple lawn furniture for my party!"

"That's a lot of painting, Abby. It's hard work. You'll probably be fed up with painting by the time you've finished the lamp."

"No," Abby insisted, "I won't be."

"Abby," her father said, "I have more experience in this than you."

"The sale ends tomorrow," the woman informed them.

Abby took a breath. "All right, I'll pay for the two gallons myself! It's my money, and I can decide what to do with it."

She laid twenty-two dollars on the counter.

The saleswoman looked at her father. "That's it, then?" she said. "You're taking the two gallons?"

"Yes!" Abby said.

"All right," her father said. He put his wallet back in his pocket. "If it's your money!"

The woman put a paid sticker on the cans of paint. "Here you are. Good luck with your project!"

Abby's father picked up the paint. They went out to the car.

Paul Hayes put the key in the ignition. He fastened his seat belt. He sighed and tapped his fingers on the steering wheel.

Suddenly, he turned toward Abby.

"Let's make a deal," he said. "I'll pay for half of the paint." He reached into his pocket, pulled out his wallet, and counted out eleven dollars.

"Really?" Abby said.

"I said I'd pay," he said. "I don't want to go back on my word."

Abby flung her arms around her father.

"You won't be sorry!" she promised. "My room will be the most beautiful you've ever seen!"

Chapter 9

What have I felt about my lamp?

1. It gives me light so I can read and write in my journal. (Thanks, lamp.)

2. It sits on my desk. (Hi.)

3. It is an ugly yellow. (Can't wait until it's rich, shiny purple!)

What about my other furniture?

1. It's in my room. (Hooray.)

2. It's white, brown, and faded blue. (Ho-hum.)

3. It is useful. (Surprise!)

No, I don't want to paint what I feel. I want to feel great after I've painted!

Paintbrush in hand, Abby surveyed her room.

She had protected her furniture and floor with drop cloths, old sheets, and newspapers. Good thing. There were drips, splatters, and brush marks everywhere!

Abby herself was covered with purple. Her old jeans and ripped-up T-shirt were smudged and smeared. Her cheek had a streak of purple on it. Her red hair now had purple highlights.

She and the room looked like a purple cyclone had passed through.

The lamp, however, had turned out beautifully. It was wet, shiny, and perfectly purple.

It looked better than Abby had ever imagined. Her whole room seemed transformed already, just by painting one lamp!

She took off the sheet covering the desk. It had once belonged to Eva. A long time ago, her father had painted it blue. An earlier green coat showed through in spots.

For a moment, she stood staring at it.

The lamp had been tricky to paint because of its curves. She had managed with a small brush and slow, steady brush strokes. The desk would be easier. It was flat and rectangular. There was only one drawer.

What would it be like to have a purple desk with a purple lamp sitting on it?

"The ultimate in purpleness," Abby said out loud. Finally, she would have a room that would shout Abby!

She stirred the paint in its can. Then she dipped a large brush in the paint and held it poised above the desk.

"Are you ready, desk?" She began to brush the deep, rich purple paint onto the desk with long, smooth strokes.

Abby pulled out the desk drawer, placed it on some newspapers, and painted it carefully. Then she painted the sides and the back of the desk, making sure not to leave any drips or bare spots.

She rested the brush on the top of the paint can and stood back to admire her handiwork.

It looked good. Okay, it looked great. She *loved* it! Her room was improved a million times over. She was probably the only girl in the fifth grade with hand-painted purple furniture!

There was a knock on the door.

"What are you painting?" Eva asked.

Isabel pinched her nose. "We can smell the fumes all the way down the hall. You think nail polish stinks? This is worse!"

"I think it smells good," Abby began, when her sisters interrupted her.

"WOW!" Isabel shrieked. "It looks *great*!"

"I love it!" Eva cried.

"Really?" Abby said. "You like it?"

"You did a terrific job," Isabel said admiringly. "No drips or glops or anything."

"I wanted to make my room unique and unforgettable," Abby explained.

"You have," Eva assured her.

"No one will ever forget your room," Isabel agreed.

Abby shook her head. Her twin sisters never praised her like this. They never even agreed!

"I might show it to my friends during the party," she confided.

"Speaking of the party," Isabel began.

"What have you planned so far?" Eva finished. "Have you thought about games? Decorations? Food?"

"Everything is organized and ready to go," Abby said. "We're eating hot dogs, chips, popcorn, potato salad, watermelon, ice cream, and cake. I wrote down games to play. Could you lend me some CDs and your CD player?"

Isabel nodded.

"Who's making the food?" Eva asked. "Who's doing the shopping? Who's baking the cakes?"

"If you want, Eva and I will help you make the cakes," Isabel offered in a friendly way.

"Um — "Abby hesitated. She had had enough of Eva and Isabel's "help" with the invitations.

"For fifty kids, you're going to need a couple of big sheet cakes," Eva said. "You also need to buy paper plates and plastic silverware. And what about drinks?"

"Oh, yeah," Abby said. "I forgot about drinks."

"You can't forget, Abby. Especially when fifty kids are running around getting thirsty." Isabel shook her head. "How many kids are actually coming?"

"Almost everyone," Abby said. She crossed her fingers. "Except Brianna and Victoria — I hope."

"They're both a pain," Eva agreed.

"If fifty kids show up," Isabel said, "you definitely need Eva and me. We'll be your own personal party consultants. Right, Eva?"

"Right, Isabel."

Abby stared at them. It wasn't very often that she saw her twin sisters agreeing like this. Had their brains been affected by the purple paint? Was it the fumes or the color?

"We'll be in charge of activities," Isabel continued.

"But shouldn't a party be like recess?" Abby cried. "Everyone can amuse themselves!"

"You're asking for trouble with that many kids," Eva said.

"We have experience," Isabel told her. "And lots of ideas."

"If you paint my desk for me," Eva said, "I'll give you all the help you want."

"Well . . ." Abby began. "Maybe."

"I'll do it for free," Isabel said, with a meaningful glance at her twin. "I don't sell my services to my little sister!"

Eva shot her a dirty look. "It's called barter!" she snapped. "There's nothing wrong with it!"

"I love painting," Abby said, trying to change the

subject. "Maybe when I'm older, I'll get a job painting houses. Don't you think I'd be good at it?"

"*Yes,*" Eva and Isabel said at the same time.

"Think about our offer," Isabel said.

"I will," Abby promised. She'd attend to the party details soon. Right now, she had something more important on her mind: her room.

Abby's twin sisters walked around the desk and lamp again.

"I love them!" Eva said again. "They're *so* fantastic!"

"Amazing," Isabel said.

"Purple splendor!" Abby said.

"That's a good name for a color," Eva said.

"Purple splendor," Abby repeated as Eva and Isabel went out the door. The words rolled off her tongue like music.

She was on a roll. Or maybe a roller. She picked up a paint roller and held it up. What could she paint next? She had barely used up any of the paint. There were almost two full gallons left!

If Abby's room looked great with a purple desk and lamp, imagine what it would look like if *everything* was purple!

Where should she start?

The bureau? Too many drawers. The chair? Too many curvy parts. The bookcase? Too many books and toys to unpack.

For a moment, Abby studied her room. She leaned down and poured a little paint into the paint tray. She moved the roller back and forth to coat it with glossy purple paint. Then she rolled it out onto an empty section of her wall.

Chapter 10

Sunday | later

"My eyes have seen what
my hand did."

—Robert Lowell

Stitch and Mend Calendar

<u>What my hand did</u>:
Painted the walls of my
room glossy purple.
Painted the bookcase.
(Ran out of paint or I
would have done the bureau and chair, too.)

<u>What my eyes have seen</u>:
Purple, purple everywhere! My room is a
sea of shining purple!

My walls are <u>very</u> purple.
It's like being inside a grape
or a giant purple box.

* * *

I will put my room in the <u>Hayes Book</u> <u>of World Records</u> for "Purplest Possible Painted Space" and "Totally Terrific Transformation of Practically Pathetic Room."

I love it! I love it! I **love** it!

<u>What my hand still has to do</u>: Clean up!!!!

Wash the brushes and rollers.
Put away paint trays and stack empty cans of paint in the garage.
Throw out newspapers and fold up sheets and drop cloths.
Take a shower and change my clothes.

<u>What my eyes still want to see</u>:
My family's reaction when they walk into the Palace of Purple!

Will they jump up and down from excitement?
Will they want their own purple rooms?

Will they decide to paint the entire house purple?

Will I be able to have a purple party?

(Note: Ask Mom if I can buy purple plates, purple cups, purple napkins, purple prizes, and purple iced cake. Too bad I didn't think of asking all the fifth-graders to come dressed in purple!)

It's almost dinnertime. I will give my family a tour after dessert.

The Purple Play
by Abby Hayes

Setting: A purple bedroom
Characters: the Hayes family: Paul, Olivia, Eva, Isabel, Alex, and Abby
Time: Sunday after dinner

As the play opens, Abby Hayes, a ten-year-old girl with curly red hair (and a few purple streaks), leads her family upstairs to her bedroom.

*   *   *

Eva: You won't believe it, Mom and Dad!

Isabel: What else did you do, Abby?

Abby (mysteriously): Oh, this and that.

Olivia Hayes: I can't wait to see it!

Paul Hayes: You used up two gallons of paint. I'm impressed. Are you sure you didn't pour it down the drain?

Abby: Ha-ha. Very funny.

Alex: Can I paint _my_ lamp, too?

Paul Hayes (groans): See what you've started?

Abby: A purple riot?

Olivia Hayes: You even cleaned up after yourself.

Abby: Yep.

The Hayes family reaches the top of the stairs. With a triumphant smile, Abby flings open the door to her room.

Abby: EXPERIENCE THE PURPLE!

Mouths fall open. Eyes glaze over. Hands fly to throats. The Hayes family gapes at the walls and furniture.

 For the first time in recorded history, both Isabel _and_ Eva are speechless.

The silence lasts for several minutes. It is finally broken by Olivia Hayes.

Olivia Hayes: Your room is so, so . . . _purple!_

Paul Hayes: The People's Purple packs a punch.

Eva: Wow. Wow. Wow.

Isabel (is having trouble breathing): Oh! It looks like you painted your walls with fingernail polish!

Abby: Exactly.

Alex: Cool! Awesome! Cool!

Olivia Hayes frowns. Paul Hayes rubs the stubble on his cheek. The Hayes parents appear to be worried.

Abby: Isn't it _great_, Mom and Dad?

Olivia Hayes: How many coats will it take to repaint it?

Paul Hayes: Probably six.

Olivia Hayes: We could tack bedsheets on the walls.

Paul Hayes: Or wallpaper it.

Olivia Hayes: How about pine panels?

Abby: Wait a minute! I don't want to change a thing! I _love_ my purple room!!!

Paul Hayes: In one week, you'll be begging for white walls.

Abby: I _won't_!

Olivia Hayes: You don't want a calm, gentle, restful shade of lilac?

Abby: No!

Paul Hayes: Can you really live with this, Abby?

Abby: Of course!

The Hayes parents turn to each other and shrug.

Olivia Hayes: It's her room, isn't it?

Paul Hayes: When she gets sick of it, she'll just have to repaint it.

Olivia Hayes: What about curtains, Abby? I hope you've changed your mind. You have enough purple in your room now.

Abby: No! There's <u>never</u> enough purple! The more, the merrier!

The play ends as Eva, Isabel, and Alex cluster around Abby, asking her to paint <u>their</u> rooms!

PURPLE PAINT FOREVER!!!!!

I am going to call all my friends and tell them.

No, I'll surprise them.

Chapter 11

Thursday

"I never think of the
future. It comes soon enough."

—*Albert Einstein*

Great Big Calendar of Time and Space

He's right!!!!!
The future is far away.
The present is right now.
I'm thinking about the present, not the
future.

The Present:

My room is magnificently
purple. Last night I painted
my bureau and chair with
more of the People's Purple
paint. Mom is making curtains
for me. They are pale lilac

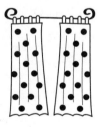

with purple polka dots. She also gave me a purple-patterned bedspread. Why should I think about the future when my present is perfectly purple???

(Note: How many "p" words did I use in the last paragraph? Purple, painted, People's, Purple, paint, pale, purple, polka dots, purple-patterned, present, perfectly, purple. If you can say that seven times very quickly without stumbling, you will win a page in the Hayes Book of World Records!)

The Future:

Eva and Isabel want me to think about the future. The future is my party. They want me to plan and prepare everything in advance. I still have more than a week to go!!! I already did some of the stuff.

Mom and I bought plastic forks, spoons, and knives, plates, napkins, and cups. We also bought ten bottles of soda and party prizes. Yes, the prizes are pencils.

So there, Eva and Isabel! I am preparing! (And adding more "p" words: Party, plan, prepare, plastic, plates, prizes, and pencils!!!)

If I listened to my "wise, experienced" twin sisters, I'd worry about the future every single second. I'm going to enjoy my perfectly purple room instead!!!!!!

Last night I hung my calendars on the walls. The pictures of animals, sunsets, oceans, and vegetables really stand out now! My calendars look exciting in my newly painted room!

"I have your essays about your rooms," Ms. Bunder announced to the fifth-graders. She held up a sheaf of papers. "I reread every single one."

Abby's stomach lurched. The room essay hadn't been one of her best. In fact, it might have been one of her worst. It had been difficult to find *anything* to say about her room last week.

Tyler raised his hand. "Why did you have to read them again? We read them out loud in class!!!"

Ms. Bunder nodded. "Reading to yourself is a different experience from having a paper read to you. Sometimes a student will mutter and swallow the words. I'll miss hearing the best parts. It can work the other way around, too. Sometimes a student with dramatic flair will give life to a poorly written piece."

Abby wondered if she had done that. Had Ms. Bunder looked at her assignment and realized it was even worse than she thought?

"Get out your writing notebooks," Ms. Bunder instructed the students. "I'll return last week's work, and then we'll get started on something new."

She went from desk to desk, handing students their papers.

"I got an A+!" Bethany squealed.

"For writing about *hamsters*?" Brianna demanded.

"It's not *what* you write about, it's *how* you write about it," Ms. Bunder told her, loud enough so the entire class could hear.

"That's not always true," Abby whispered to Natalie. "My room was boring so I wrote a boring essay about it."

Natalie shook her head. "You're wrong. I liked your essay."

Abby shrugged. Natalie was a loyal friend. But *she* was the one who was wrong.

Ms. Bunder handed Brianna her paper. "Not bad, Brianna."

"Not bad?" Brianna repeated in disbelief. She glanced at her paper. Her face turned red.

"Ms. Bunder! I deserve better than a B!" she cried. "No one else in the fifth grade has a large-screen television in their bedroom!"

"Brianna, I'm not grading you on equipment," Ms. Bunder said.

"Why not?" Brianna demanded.

Ms. Bunder ignored her.

"Hey, look at this!" Mason yelled, pointing to his paper. Ms. Bunder had marked it with a large A.

"Congratulations," Abby said. Mason had an A; Bethany had an A+; Brianna had a B. Was this going to be Abby's first C in creative writing?

Abby wanted to jump up and tell everyone that her room was now completely transformed; that she had sanded and scraped and painted all weekend; and that she now had a purple lamp, bureau, chair, bookcase, and curtains.

But she wanted to surprise her friends, too. She didn't want to give away her secret before she figured out the perfect way to reveal it.

"Abby," Ms. Bunder said. "Here you go."

Abby flipped the paper over fast before she could see the grade. "I can't look," she said to Natalie.

"You tell me what it is."

Natalie turned the paper over. "B+," she announced.

"Really?"

"B+," Natalie repeated firmly.

Abby opened her eyes. She looked down at her paper. "Wow!" she cried. "B+! That's *good*."

"I told you!" Natalie said. " 'It's not what you write about, it's how you write about it,' " she repeated.

"It's better than I thought," Abby said. She leaned toward Natalie.

Abby *had* to tell *someone* about her room. "Guess what," she began.

"What?" Natalie asked.

Ms. Bunder clapped her hands for the students' attention. She picked up a piece of chalk. "Who has ever written a What I Did on My Summer Vacation essay?" she asked.

"It's nothing," Abby whispered to Natalie as the entire class raised their hands. "I'll tell you later."

Ms. Bunder smiled. "Today we'll write something a little different. We'll write a What I'd *Like* to Do on My Summer Vacation essay."

"Huh?" Mason said.

"If you could do *anything*," Ms. Bunder explained, "what would you do on summer vacation?"

"Read joke books," Rachel said.

"Camp out under the stars for three months!" Jessica said.

"Work in an animal hospital!" Bethany cried.

Dozens of voices broke out at once.

"I want to go swimming!" "Visit my cousins!" "Watch a lot of TV!" "Go to Paris!" "Do nothing!"

Ms. Bunder held up her hand for quiet. "The sky's the limit," she said. "Write about how you would spend an ideal summer vacation. It doesn't matter if it's on Mars or at the New Jersey shore."

Abby and Natalie exchanged glances.

"Hogwarts," Natalie said. She grabbed a pen and paper.

"Nonstop computer games!" Zach yelled.

"Write it down," Ms. Bunder instructed. "How would it feel to play computer games all day and all night? Is that *really* your ideal summer vacation?"

Abby looked down at the blank paper. No ideas came to mind. She silently reread the ending to her last week's assignment.

"I wish I had a purple billowy ceiling! I wish I had a purple rug and purple curtains! I wish I could turn my room into a Palace of Purple!"

A week ago, this had been just a dream. Now it was reality.

I did it, she said to herself. *I really DID turn my room into a Palace of Purple! And got a B+ on an essay that I didn't think was very good.*

If she imagined something wonderful for her summer vacation, would it really happen?

Now that she had transformed her room, what was left?

Abby thought. She might attend a writer's workshop for kids. Throw the best party that the fifth grade had ever seen. Go on an airplane by herself and visit Grandma Emma. Learn to play the piano.

That was just the beginning.

She picked up her pen and began to write.

Chapter 12

Friday | after school

"Time works wonders."

Hourglass Calendar

I wish it did! I'd love to have time work wonders. It would be great if time shopped for my party, made the food, put up the decorations, and chose the music. How can I get time to do that?

I need <u>someone</u> to work wonders! I've been so busy thinking about my room, I haven't even thought about my party.

The party is tomorrow! Fifty-one kids are showing up. Everyone is coming, even Brianna and Victoria.

(We pause for a moment of silent screaming.)

* * *

I'm not ready. I'm not even close to ready. What about food? What about tables? What about games? What about decorations? And music? Time isn't helping at all! It's bringing me closer and closer to my party.

Eva and Isabel were right. I should have prepared in advance. I should have accepted their help. Is it too late? Will they still help me?

Abby slammed her journal shut, jumped up from her bed, and went to find her father.

"Dad!" she called, running up the stairs to his home office. "Are you there?"

He didn't answer. No one else was home. Her mother was still at work. Her twin sisters were still at school. Eva had lacrosse practice; Isabel had drama club. Alex was at a friend's house.

"Dad!" Abby yelled. *"Dad!"*

"I'm here!" Paul Hayes appeared at the bottom of the stairs. "What's the matter, Abby? You sound desperate!"

"I am! My party is tomorrow!" Abby wailed.

"Nothing's ready! Except my room," she added. "I should have had everything done by now!"

"Calm down," her father said. "You're not in this alone. No one expects you to throw a party for the entire fifth grade by yourself. Your mother and I haven't forgotten that fifty-one hungry ten-year-olds will descend on the house tomorrow at two P.M. No way!"

Paul Hayes took a piece of paper out of his pocket. He unfolded it and began to read. "Twenty packages of hot dogs and rolls, ten bags of chips, popcorn, three gallons of ice cream, a bucket of potato salad, six bottles of juice, five watermelons . . ."

He looked at Abby. "That's the shopping list. All right?"

Abby nodded.

Her father continued. "We'll go shopping after dinner. While we're at the supermarket, your mother will haul out the tables, the tent, bowls, and serving utensils. Your sisters are baking the cakes."

"*Together?*" Abby cried in dismay.

"Even the twins occasionally cooperate," Paul Hayes said. "Though I admit I haven't seen it often."

"What if they start fighting and burn the cake?

What if they forget to put in baking powder? What if they use salt instead of sugar?"

"If you're that worried, why don't you bake the cakes?" her father suggested. "You'll have to do it after shopping, decorating, and setting up tables."

"Eva and Isabel can bake them!" Abby said quickly. "I just hope they don't ruin everything!"

"It'll turn out fine," her father reassured her. "You can count on your sisters to bake two delicious cakes."

"Tasting is believing," Abby muttered.

Her father put his hand on her shoulder. "What do you have left to do?"

"Just decorating, blowing up balloons, finding music, planning a few games, making sure everyone has a good time, and cleaning up afterward."

"You'll get through it," her father promised. "So will we."

Abby unloaded the groceries from the car.

"Did you and your dad get everything?" her mother asked, pushing back a stray lock of hair from her face. She was pulling serving utensils out of a drawer.

"Yes," Abby said.

"Eggs?" Isabel asked. "Cream cheese? Confectioner's sugar? Eva and I need them for the frostings."

"I think so," Abby said. She rummaged in one of the bags and pulled out a carton of eggs and a package of cream cheese. "Here's some of it, anyway. What are you making?"

"I'm making a carrot cake with cream cheese frosting," Eva announced, pointing to a stainless steel bowl full of batter. "And Isabel is making a double chocolate cake with creamy vanilla frosting."

"Yum!" Abby said. "Can I lick the bowls?"

"No way!" Isabel said. "Get out of here! Don't disturb the chefs!"

"Here, Abby." Eva poured the batter into a large pan, then scraped the bowl with a spatula that she offered to her younger sister. "You can taste this."

"Don't!" Isabel warned. "You might get sick from the raw eggs!"

Abby hesitated.

"You don't want to be ill the night before your party," her mother agreed. "Put that in the dishwasher, Eva."

"*I* licked it," Eva said. "It's delicious."

"If you throw up all night and have a fever,

don't expect any sympathy from me," Isabel said.

"I never expect any sympathy from you, anyway," Eva retorted. She held out the spatula to Abby. "Sure you don't want a taste?"

Abby shook her head. "I don't think so." She put the packages of hot dogs into the refrigerator. The last thing she needed was food poisoning.

Eva put the pan into the oven. "Only one hour, and the carrot cake will be ready!" she announced.

"Hooray!" Abby said.

Isabel was emptying her bowl into another pan. "This is going to be the best chocolate cake you've ever tasted," she promised Abby. "Do you know what the secret is?"

"What?" Abby asked. "Coconut? Orange flavoring? Cherries?"

"Vinegar," Isabel announced.

"Vinegar?" Abby cried. "Are you crazy?"

"Nope," Isabel said, sliding the pan into the oven and setting the timer. "This cake will be delicious."

"Mom! She'll ruin my party!" Abby cried. "Do something!"

"She'll ruin it," Eva agreed. "Isabel ruins everything."

Isabel stuck her tongue out at her twin.

Olivia Hayes paused at the sink, where she was

filling ice cube trays with water. "Stop it, Eva and Isabel. Stop tormenting your sister." She turned to Abby. "It's a perfectly good recipe. I've made it many times myself. The cake is excellent."

"Are you *sure*?" Abby asked anxiously. Vinegar cake sounded like a nightmare. She could already see her friends and classmates puckering up.

"If it isn't, I'll get a cake from the bakery," her mother promised. "Now let's set up the folding tables on the back porch."

Alex ran into the kitchen in his pajamas. "I want to help, too! Can I bake a cake?"

"They're already done," Eva said, affectionately ruffling his hair.

"They smell good," Alex said.

Abby looked in one of the bags. "Alex! Do you want to blow up some balloons?" she asked him. "I'm going to tie them on the back porch and fence."

Alex nodded his head.

"Here." Abby handed him a package of purple balloons. "Be sure to tie them tight so the air won't leak out," she instructed him.

"I *know*!" Alex said.

Abby followed her mother onto the back porch. Together they set up the folding tables.

"We'll put tablecloths on them tomorrow," her mother said. "We don't want them blowing away overnight."

"No!" Abby agreed. She already had vinegar cake. She didn't want runaway tablecloths, too.

She looked up at the sky. It was filled with clouds. Another thing to worry about. "What if the weather's bad?" she asked. "What if it's cold or pouring?"

Olivia Hayes shook her head. "I'm rooting for blue skies. If we have fifty kids in the house . . ." Her voice trailed off.

"We could go down to the basement," Abby suggested. "We could rent movies and play Ping-Pong."

"The basement will hold twenty people, maximum," her mother said. "We'd have to divide the party. Put half in the living room and half downstairs."

"And some in my room!" Abby said.

Her mother frowned. "I don't want the entire fifth grade running wild in the house. We better keep our fingers crossed."

"Okay," Abby said. "I'll cross my toes, too."

The smell of freshly baked cakes filled the house. Eva and Isabel were preparing frostings as the sheet cakes cooled on the countertops.

"My cream cheese frosting is a lot healthier than yours," Eva said, casting a critical eye on Isabel's bowl. "Yours is all sugar."

"Guess whose cake is going to be the most popular?" Isabel retorted.

"Just don't tell anyone the ingredients!" Eva said.

"No one will know," Isabel said. "And everyone will want seconds!"

"I hope so," Abby said, coming into the kitchen with Alex, who was still blowing up balloons.

"Don't worry," her father said. He was carrying bags of charcoal and a grill for the hot dogs.

Abby looked around at the kitchen. The sink was filled with bowls. The table was stacked with party food and utensils. A few stray balloons lay on the floor. There were to-do lists on the refrigerator and dirty forks and spoons on the countertops.

"That's all anyone says!" she cried. "Don't worry! Don't worry! Why should I stop worrying? The entire fifth grade will be here tomorrow!"

"She has party panic," Isabel said, stirring the frosting with a spoon.

"Wait until you've thrown four or five parties in a row," Eva said. "It'll get a lot easier."

Her father set down the charcoal and grill by the

back door. "I told you, Abby. You're not alone. You've got plenty of people helping you."

Alex knotted a string on a purple balloon to tie on the front door. "Yeah, Abby," he agreed. "Like me."

Her father dusted off his hands. "We'll give you more help tomorrow."

Abby took a deep breath. "You're right, Dad," she said, looking around at her family. "Thanks, everyone!"

"We'll make you pay later," Eva joked.

"Yeah, wait until *our* next party," Isabel said.

In her room, Abby lay back on her bed and gazed at her purple walls. She sighed with satisfaction, then reached for her journal and opened it up.

Time didn't work wonders, but my family did!

Hayes Family Wonder Workers:
1. Dad. Bought food, set up grill, will make hot dogs tomorrow.
2. Mom. Got out folding tables. Took out tablecloths. Stacked paper plates, plastic silverware,

napkins, and cups on tables. Made extra ice cubes. Got out serving utensils, juice pitchers, and cutting boards. Found crepe paper for decorations.

    3. Isabel. Baked chocolate (vinegar) cake and frosted it.

    4. Eva. Baked carrot cake and frosted it. Wrote "Hooray! It's Summer!" on both cakes in purple icing.

    5. Alex. Blew up one package of purple balloons. Tied balloon to front door so friends can find party.

    6. Abby. Thought of party. Won argument with parents. Planned and printed invitations. Painted room purple. Went shopping with Dad. Put away food. Helped Mom carry out tables. Drew stars, hearts, and squiggles on both cakes to decorate. Blew up some balloons.

Are we ready? Almost!!!!!!!

Chapter 13

Saturday

"Tomorrow never comes."

Calendar of Days

Yes, it does! Tomorrow is here! It's today!

Today is my party. Soon my classmates will be here!

HOORAY!!!

Abby looked out the front window. "When will they arrive?" she asked impatiently.

Isabel smiled. "Not for at least another ten minutes," she said. "And people usually come late, anyway."

The tables were set up for the party. There were

platters of cheese and rolls and fruit. There were bowls of popcorn and gallons of soda. The cakes were iced and decorated and hidden in the refrigerator.

The yard was ready, too. Alex had plugged in the boom box and stacked a pile of CDs next to it. The volleyball net stretched across the back of the yard. Abby had dragged out a trunk full of games. There were balloons tied to the fence and the back porch.

Abby walked over to the mirror and stared anxiously at her reflection. She was wearing a purple T-shirt and purple-flowered pants. There were purple barrettes in her hair, and she wore sneakers with purple daisies.

"You look cute," Isabel said. "Are you going to show everyone your purple room?"

Abby shook her head. "No."

She had decided to invite Jessica, Natalie, and Bethany — and maybe Casey — to see it at the end of the party. "Only my close friends."

A car door slammed. There were footsteps on the front porch.

"Someone's here," Isabel said just as the doorbell rang.

Abby ran to answer it. "It's Jessica and Sarah!" she cried. "You're our first guests!"

Jessica handed her a platter of cookies. "These are for the party," she said. "My mother and I made them this morning."

"Thanks!" Abby said.

Sarah shifted uncomfortably on the front steps. "I didn't bring anything," she said. "I hope that's okay."

"We have *plenty* of food," Abby told her.

"Wait until you taste my chocolate cake!" Isabel called.

"Great!" Jessica said.

"It better be," Abby said under her breath.

"What?" Sarah asked.

Abby didn't answer. "The party's in the back-yard," she said instead. "I'll show you the way."

"I *know* where it is!" Jessica reminded her. "I've only been here a million times since kindergarten."

"Oh, yeah, right," Abby said.

"If you want to go out back with your friends, I'll answer the bell," Isabel offered.

"Thanks, sis," Abby said. She led her friends through the house.

The entire fifth grade of Lancaster Elementary was gathered in the Hayes backyard.

The boys stood on one side. The girls stood on the other.

Led by Mason, the boys were having a burping contest. Tyler was burping the alphabet. Zach was cheering him on. Casey was claiming he could burp "Twinkle, Twinkle" and "When You Wish Upon a Star." Jonathan was betting he couldn't.

The girls were clustered around Brianna and Victoria, who were describing the Tiffany Crystal concert the night before.

"We had front-row seats," Brianna bragged. "My cousin got us the best tickets. Right, Bethany?"

Bethany was silent.

"Too bad you couldn't come," Victoria snickered.

"I only had two tickets," Brianna explained. "Of *course* I had to give one to Victoria. You understand, don't you, Bethany?"

"Well, actually, I — " Bethany began.

"Who cares?" Victoria interrupted. "The concert was great. I got, like, tons of cool stuff. A poster, two new CDs — "

"I bought an authentic Tiffany Crystal key chain," Brianna bragged.

"I don't — " Bethany tried to say.

"Tiffany Crystal was, like, totally awesome," Victoria continued. "The singing and dancing were the best. I, like, *love* her song "Nasty Sugar Sweet — "

Brianna and Victoria linked arms and burst into song.

"Someone shut them up," Natalie moaned. "Please!"

"I'll do it!" Abby's little brother Alex offered. He scampered onto the porch, put a CD in the boom box, and turned the volume up full blast.

Victoria and Brianna broke off their singing.

"Like, *what?*" Victoria said.

"The Bumble Boys!" Brianna cried. "Are you serious?"

"They're the bomb," Alex said.

"I, like, totally hate the Bumble Boys," Victoria said. "Can you put on some Tiffany Crystal?"

"Sorry," Abby said, "I don't have any Tiffany."

"This is a Tiffany-free zone," Natalie said.

Victoria rolled her eyes. "Why am I, like, here, instead of at the mall?"

Brianna cast a quick glance in the direction of the boys. Mason let out an enormous burp.

"They are so immature!" Brianna shrieked. "Why didn't you take my advice, Abby, and invite the sixth- and seventh-grade boys instead?"

"Eeeeuuu!" Rachel said. "They're even *worse*!"

"No, they're not," Brianna disagreed.

"Boys are boring," Bethany said suddenly in a loud voice. "I like hamsters better. Sometimes I like them better than girls, too."

Everyone stared at her.

"What?" Tyler yelled. "She prefers hamsters to people?"

"She *lives* in a hamster cage," Victoria said nastily.

Bethany's eyes widened. Her face got red. Her lip wobbled.

"My room doesn't smell," Victoria sneered.

"Blondie doesn't smell any worse than you or Brianna!" Bethany retorted.

There was a moment of shocked silence. Then suddenly everyone was arguing.

Tyler and Zach were yelling that girls were worse than boys. Rachel and Natalie were yelling that boys were worse than girls. Victoria was yelling at Brianna that it was time to leave the party. Brianna was yelling at Bethany that it was her fault. Bethany was yelling that she hated Victoria. Mason was burping. Jonathan and Megan were high-fiving each other, although no one knew why. Sarah and Jessica yelled for someone to turn down the music.

The Bumble Boys were blaring.

The Hayes backyard was a scene of pandemonium.

Abby looked around frantically for help. Isabel and Eva were nowhere in sight. Alex was fiddling with the CD player, turning the volume up and down. Her parents were getting food from the kitchen.

"Stop! Stop, everyone!" Abby cried wildly. She ran from one person to another, trying to get them to stop fighting.

No one listened.

As suddenly as it had begun, the fight ended. Bethany wiped the tears from her eyes and started to shoot hoops with Jessica and Sarah. A group of boys and girls went over to the volleyball net. Brianna reapplied colored lip gloss.

"At least there's music," Victoria grumbled. She began to dance to the music of the Bumble Boys.

Paul and Olivia Hayes came out of the house with a big bowl of potato salad and packages of hot dogs. Abby's father fired up the grill.

"Nice party, honey," he said to Abby. "Everyone's having a good time."

"Uh, yeah," Abby said. "Sure, Dad."

* * *

The fifth-graders had just finished eating hot dogs, potato salad, chips, and watermelon when Isabel and Eva carried out the cakes.

"Happy end of school year to you!" they sang. "Happy end of school year to you! Have a great summer vacation — and eat lots of cake, too!"

Abby's twin sisters set the cakes down on a table.

"This is my extraordinary carrot cake with cream cheese icing," Eva announced.

"And this is my fabulous chocolate cake with vanilla icing," Isabel said. "With the mystery ingredient."

She picked up a toy horn and tooted on it.

"We are now serving cake," the twins announced in unison.

The fifth-graders rushed toward the tables.

Abby took a piece of Eva's cake and a piece of Isabel's. With her fork, she pried loose a tiny crumb of Isabel's mystery chocolate cake. Carefully, she put it in her mouth. She closed her eyes and tasted.

"It's good!" she said in surprise.

"*Told* you!" Isabel smirked.

"Have you tasted mine?" Eva demanded. "It's even better!"

Abby took a large forkful of carrot cake. "It's delicious, too!"

"They're both great," Jessica agreed.

"Yuh," Casey agreed, his mouth full of cake.

"I wish this party would never end!" Natalie said.

"Me, too," Jonathan agreed.

"Can I have second helpings?" Tyler asked.

"What about thirds?" Mason demanded.

Victoria made a face. "Piggy, piggy."

"This cake is good, but the cake my mother ordered from the French bakery was even better," Brianna said. *"Eh bien, c'est vrai, n'est-ce pas?"*

"Speak English!" Natalie said. "No one understands a word you're saying!"

"Thank goodness," Abby said under her breath.

Bethany snickered.

"Tant pis," Brianna said. "Too bad. If you're all ignorant — " She stood up to throw out her paper plate.

"Another game of volleyball?" Abby suggested.

"Great idea! Yeah! Let's do it!" Her classmates got up and ran over to the net.

The party was going as smoothly as possible, Abby thought with satisfaction. The games were fun, the food was great — even the vinegar cake! — and all the fifth-graders were laughing and having a good time.

Abby hadn't needed Isabel and Eva's party-planning services, after all. She was just a natural party-giver.

She picked up the volleyball and served it over the net.

"Eeeeeeeeee!" The first shriek came from Brianna.

"Aaaaaaaaaaa!" The second came from Victoria.

Fat, wet, purple water balloons were exploding in front of the two best-dressed girls in the fifth grade.

They flung their arms up to protect themselves, but they were already drenched from head to toe. Their sequined scoop-necked T-shirts, shiny short skirts, and bump-toed shoes were dripping wet. Their hair hung in soggy tangles. Mascara ran down their faces.

Brianna was screaming helplessly. "My best shirt! My best skirt! My best hair!"

"I'm, like, totally soaked!" Victoria moaned.

"It's the bomb!" Mason cackled as another water balloon splattered in front of Victoria.

Suddenly, the air was filled with water balloons. Megan, Rachel, Bethany, and Natalie were the new targets.

"Ha-ha-ha-ha-ha!" laughed Mason, Tyler, and Zach.

Shrieking and yelling, the girls ran around the yard, dodging water balloons. The balloons splattered near the food tables and the volleyball net. They splattered by the garden and on the grill.

Natalie stopped.

"Revenge!" she cried, running for the hose. "*War!*"

The girls flocked behind her.

Natalie brandished the hose. "Girls against boys! To the wet, sloppy end!"

"Hooray!" the girls shouted. "War on boys!"

Natalie aimed the hose at Mason, then doused Tyler and Zach.

"Let's get them!" Bethany cried, emptying a soda bottle on Jonathan's head.

"Stop! Stop! Stop!" Abby screamed, but no one listened.

Her party was racing out of control. She looked around for her parents — or even Eva and Isabel — but they had all gone inside. Alex was the only Hayes in sight.

Chapter 14

Saturday

"When the going gets rough,
remember to keep calm."

—Horace

Choppy Water Calendar

Oh, yeah? I'd like to see <u>anyone</u> keep calm when purple water balloons are flying through the air and the garden hose is turned full force on the boys!

I didn't keep calm. I was screaming like everyone else. My parents didn't hear us. Was it because we had the CD player on full blast?

No one else heard me, either.

Abby watched helplessly as Tyler got Bethany with a

water balloon and Bethany squirted him with the hose. Jessica had filled a watering can and was sprinkling Mason.

Everything was getting soaked: kids, tables, food — potato chips and popcorn, a few hot dog rolls, and the last pieces of the "Hooray! It's Summer!" cakes.

Fifth-graders were running all over the yard. Flowers were trampled. The ground was muddy. The crepe paper decorations stained the tablecloths with purple dye.

"This has to stop!" Abby cried.

If her parents saw this, they'd forbid her to ever have another party.

It was only a matter of time before they came outside again and saw the battlefield.

What could she do? Was there a bullhorn somewhere on the porch? Or an electric switch that would turn off the fighting? Or —

Abby ran down the porch steps and around to the side of the house. She found the water spigot and turned off the water. Then she unscrewed the hose.

"Hey! What happened? There isn't any more water!" Loud, disappointed cries came from the girls.

"Awwwwwwww!" The boys yelled. The last water balloons were gone.

A crowd of drenched, dripping fifth-graders stood in the Hayes backyard.

The boys looked at the girls. They girls looked at the boys.

"Now what?" Bethany asked.

There was nothing left to eat. The food was water-logged.

There was nothing left to do. The games were wet.

There was nothing left to say.

The mood of the party was dreary and dim.

Was this how it was going to end?

Abby stood on the porch steps and surveyed the ruins of her party.

What now?

She clapped her hands for attention. The fifth-graders turned toward her.

"Announcing — "Abby began. She stopped. What was she announcing, anyway?

"For the final thirty-five minutes of the party" — she checked her watch — "for the final thirty-*seven* minutes of the party — "

"Get to the point!" Zach yelled.

"We will, um, we will — "

"Dry off?" Casey suggested.

The fifth-graders began to laugh.

"We will — " Abby began again. She had to think of *something*.

"Like, change our clothes?" Victoria suggested nastily.

"I don't have a changing room." Abby began. Her eyes lit up. "I just have a changed room!"

She took a deep breath.

"You are all invited on a tour of Abby's room!" she announced. "You are invited to see Abby's Spectacular Palace of Purple."

"Palace of Purple?" Natalie said. "I thought your room was white. With lots of calendars."

"Yes, there are lots of calendars," Abby agreed. "But in the last few weeks, I have painted the entire room — walls, furniture, and lamps — a rich, glorious purple."

Jessica's mouth dropped open.

"You did?" Natalie said. "And you didn't tell us!"

"Her room is awesome!" Alex cried.

Now she had her classmates' attention.

"Come experience the purple!" she cried. "I've transformed my dull, dingy room into a purple poem!"

*   *   *

The fifth-graders were lined up in the hallway outside Abby's bedroom. The line extended down the stairs and through the living room.

"Step right up! Come right in! Don't push or shove!" Abby called. "No admission charged for the Tour de Room!"

"One at a time," Casey said. He stood at the door next to Abby, making sure that kids didn't crowd in.

"This is *so* cool," Bethany said, gazing at the shiny purple.

"It's actually hot," Abby said. "I matched it to Isabel's hot purple fingernail polish."

"You did it yourself?" Zach asked admiringly. "Your parents didn't help you?"

"I did it *all*," Abby said proudly.

"It's like living inside a purple-tronic machine," Tyler said.

"What's that?" Abby asked. "I want one."

"A machine that manufactures the color purple." Tyler shrugged. "I just made it up."

Jonathan stepped inside the room. "Wow!" he yelled. "Purple power!"

Abby smiled.

"Purple Peter Piper picked a purple peck of pickled

purple peppers," Casey said to Jonathan. "Can you say that five times in a row?"

"No," Jonathan said.

"Purple Peter Piper picked a purple peck of pickled purple peppers," Casey repeated. "Purple to the max!"

"I can't believe your parents let you do this," Natalie said. "Mine would never let me."

"They weren't too happy about it," Abby confessed. "But it was too late!"

Brianna and Victoria entered the room.

"Welcome to the Palace of Purple," Abby said.

"*My* room is painted peach, with plaster molding and silk-striped wallpaper," Brianna bragged. "My mother hired an interior decorator. I have a Belgian lace canopy bed. It looks like a *real* princess room."

"Do you call this Putrid Purple?" Victoria snickered. "Or Purple Pimple?"

Mason made a rude noise. "I like it," he said. "It's loud. It's bright. It's — "

"Purple?" Zach finished for him.

Victoria's lip curled. "It's — "

"*Perfect*," Bethany finished for her.

"Was I, like, talking to you?" Victoria asked.

"Probably not," Bethany said. "Who cares?"

Victoria opened her mouth and shut it again.

"Congratulations, Abby," Brianna said. "On your party and the purple room. Victoria and I think it's *très belle*." She checked her watch. "I think my mother will be picking us up soon."

"Dingdong," Natalie said as the two of them swept out of the room.

"Good riddance to bad rubbish," Bethany muttered.

Her friends stared at her.

"Are you *serious*?" Natalie said.

Bethany nodded.

"Hooray!" Abby and Natalie said in unison.

"Do you think I should invite Ms. Bunder to see my room?" Abby asked. "Her assignment made me decide to paint."

"Sure," Jessica said. "Why not?"

"Maybe it'll give her an idea for another creative writing assignment!" Abby exclaimed. "She gets ideas from unexpected places!"

"I bet she'll love it," Bethany said.

Rachel peered into the room. "Let me guess," she said. "Your favorite color is — "

Chapter 15

> **Sunday**
>
> "You can't have too much of a good thing."
>
> *Woolly Mammoth Calendar*

True or False?

1. You can't have too much purple!

2. You can't have too many kids at a party!

3. You can't have too much cake!

4. You can't have too many water balloons!

5. You can't have too many friends tour your room!

6. You can't have too much of Brianna and Victoria.

Answers:

1. True
2. True
3. True
4. False
5. True
6. False (If you got this one wrong, you are either Brianna or Victoria.)

<u>The party is over!</u>

Boo-hoo! How did it happen so fast?

Tomorrow, which became today, is now yesterday.

(If you can figure out what that means, you win a piece of leftover party cake! It only got a <u>little</u> wet.)

The cleanup is done.

I threw out all the paper plates and cups. I also threw out the soggy hot dog buns and the soaked decorations. I recycled the soda bottles and the plastic silverware. I put the tablecloths in the washing machine. I

dried off the games. I
reconnected the hose. I mopped
the kitchen floor where my friends
had tracked in mud. I picked up
billions of broken balloon pieces from
the yard.

Party Facts:

Watermelons eaten: 3½

Water balloons thrown: 34

Tiffany Crystal CDs played: 0 (ha-ha-ha-ha)

Hayes Book of World Records broken: 5

1. Abby wins an award for "Fastest
Thinking During Fierce Fighting."

2. Mason wins for "Sneakiest Balloon
Bombing."

3. Victoria and Brianna win for "Soggiest
Outfits."

4. Bethany wins for "Bravest Comeback."

5. My family wins the "Highest Hayes
Helper" Award! They are the best!

   (They even helped me with the cleanup.)

The Hayes Family Discusses Abby's Party:

Olivia Hayes: Looks like your first party was a huge success, Abby.

Eva: Beginner's luck! You didn't have a single disaster, did you?

Abby: Uh . . .

Isabel: They liked the purple pencil party favors, didn't they?

Abby: I handed them out in my purple room.

Olivia Hayes: They'll remember the party when they write with the pencils.

Isabel: Or when they see anything purple.

Abby: I hope so!

Alex: The water balloon fight was the best!

Paul Hayes: What water balloon fight?

Abby: Uh . . .

Eva: So when are you planning the next party, Abby?

Abby: In five years?

French Dictionary (otherwise known as my older sister Isabel Hayes):

Eh bien, c'est vrai, n'est-ce pas? Well,

that's true, isn't it?

Tant pis (the "s" is silent!): Too bad

Très belle: very beautiful

(Did Brianna really say that about my room? No wonder she said it in French! She didn't want anyone to know! Maybe she liked my Purple Palace better than her designer bedroom. I bet she did!!!!!!)

I love my purple room! I love it so much!!!! So do a lot of kids. I can't wait to invite everyone over again. I will expand my circle of friends. We will all enjoy the Purple Palace together!

Not all at once! The Hayes family won't see long lines waiting on the stairs for a peek at the purple. I will invite ONLY two or three friends at a time!

The AMAZING DAYS of ABBY HAYES

Out of Sight, Out of Mind

To <u>You</u>
All the readers and friends of Abby!!

Chapter 1

Monday

"What goes up, must come down."

Stock Market Calendar

Noooooooooo!

Every night I've been studying math facts for half an hour. Last week I got my first A on a math quiz!!!! Ms. Kantor told me if I keep it up, I might get a B+ on my next report card. Wow! Hooray!

My math grade is going up. MUST it come down???? NO! NO! _NO!_

This quote is true for:
—balloons
—airplanes

—birds

—eyebrows

This quote is not true for:
—Abby's math grade
—Abby's ability to add, subtract, multiply, and divide
—Abby's happiness quotient

Don't believe everything you read in calendars. Even if you have the world's biggest collection. Even if calendars cover the walls of your room and are stacked in piles in your closet.

"I have candy bars in my backpack," Jessica said. She unzipped the pack and took out a plastic bag. "Want one?"

"No eating in my room," Abby said. "We can go downstairs."

Jessica looked at her best friend in surprise. "You never used to mind."

"That was before I painted my room purple," Abby explained, gesturing toward the shiny purple walls and furniture in her room.

Abby had coated everything in the room with her favorite color: walls, desk, bureau, chair, and lamp. Her sister Eva had sewed purple polka-dotted curtains for the windows, and her sister Isabel had donated a purple spread for the bed. Now her room was a Palace of Purple.

Everything was purple except for the floor!

"Okay," Jessica said. She swung the bag of chocolate bars back and forth. "Let's go. It's left over from Halloween."

"Yum," Abby said.

The two girls went downstairs.

On the landing, Abby stopped to pet T-Jeff. The kitten rubbed his face against her leg and purred.

"I wish I could pet him," Jessica said longingly. "I'm so allergic to cats."

"So is Alex," Abby said, referring to her younger brother. "Isabel and I have to take turns vacuuming the living room every day."

Isabel and Abby shared ownership of T-Jeff. He was originally Abby's kitten, but she hadn't been able to take care of him by herself. Her older sister had taken over most of the work. She had also insisted on naming the kitten Thomas Jefferson. Abby had shortened it to T-Jeff.

"His name sounds like a new kind of dinosaur," Jessica commented.

"Tyrannosaurus Jefferson," Abby joked. "The kitten that strikes fear into the hearts of dust balls, mice, strings, and yarn."

They crossed the living room where Abby's brother, Alex, was watching a show on TV. In the dining room, schoolbooks were stacked on the table. The smell of cooking came from the kitchen.

"Hi, Jessica. Good to see you." Abby's father, Paul Hayes, was standing at the stove, stirring a pot of chili. "Can you stay for dinner tonight?"

Jessica shook her head. "No thanks, I can't. My mom and I are getting Chinese food tonight."

"Any special occasion?" Paul Hayes asked.

Jessica nodded. She took out two chocolate bars and gave one to Abby. She unwrapped her own and took a bite from it.

"Yes, it's a special occasion," she said after a moment. She took a breath. "It's sort of a celebration. I'm going to visit my father."

"You are?" Abby cried. "When????"

Jessica hadn't seen her father for a long time, although he called and wrote her regularly.

"Soon," Jessica said. "As soon as he enrolls me in

school. Maybe by next week. That's the end of the cycle."

Abby stared at her best friend. She couldn't utter a word. "You're going to school there?" she finally said.

"It's only for one marking period," Jessica said. "Three months. I'll be back in the spring."

Paul Hayes lowered the gas under the chili pot and put down the wooden spoon. "When did this happen, Jessica?" he asked gently.

"Last week," Jessica said. "My dad called my mother and offered to send a plane ticket. He just got married. He wants me to get to know his new family."

"He got married?" Abby cried. "Why didn't you tell me!"

"I don't know." Jessica shrugged and looked away. "His new wife has two daughters," she finally said.

"You have stepsisters?" Abby said in disbelief. "And you didn't say anything?"

Jessica was an only child. She had always been envious of Abby's brother and twin sisters. She had always wanted siblings of her own.

"They're ten and seven — just like you and Alex," Jessica said, as if that explained her silence.

"When did you last see your dad?" Paul Hayes asked.

Jessica broke off another piece of her candy bar. "Four years ago. Before he moved to Oregon."

"That's a long trip," Paul Hayes commented. "But four years is a long time not to see your father."

"Yes," Abby agreed. Was that why Jessica hadn't said anything to her? She couldn't imagine not seeing her father for four years. She'd miss him if he left for four days!

"I've never been on a plane before," Jessica confessed.

"Are you flying by yourself?" Abby asked. She glanced at her father. She had asked her parents to let her fly unaccompanied to Grandma Emma's house. They had always said no.

Jessica shook her head. "Someone's going to meet me when I change planes in Chicago."

The three of them were quiet for a moment.

"A plane trip to Oregon, a different school, a visit with your father, a stepmother, and two new siblings — anything else?" Paul Hayes asked. "Any more changes planned?"

"No." Jessica smiled.

"That's enough!" Abby cried.

There was a silence.

"What are your stepsisters' names?" Abby asked.

"Danielle and Dakota." Jessica searched in the pocket of her overalls. "I guess I forgot the picture. Danielle is our age. I'll be in class with her. She sounds pretty nice."

"At least she's not named after a state, like her sister," Abby said. "What if your parents named you Rhode Island? Or Vermont? Or Illinois? Or *Massachusetts*?"

"Massachusetts Hayes. That has a ring to it," Abby's father said. "I wish your mother and I had thought of it when you were born."

"Dad!" Abby protested.

"She gets her sense of humor from me," Paul Hayes said to Jessica. He took the salad spinner from the cupboard. "Abby, will you get the lettuce out of the refrigerator?"

Abby searched in the vegetable bin. "Can we put olives and carrots in the salad?" she asked.

"Of course." Her father nodded. "Your mother is going to miss you," he said to Jessica.

"She's taking a trip to Greece," Jessica said.

"Wonderful!" Paul Hayes said. "I wonder if we have any relatives who will take Isabel, Eva, Abby, and Alex for a month or two?"

"Dad!" Abby cried.

"It won't be easy." Her father winked at the two girls. "No sane person would take all of you for more than an hour!"

Abby glanced at Jessica to see how she was taking her father's humor. Jessica was smiling.

"I hope my dad is as nice as yours," she said as she and Abby headed back to Abby's room.

"It's funny — " Abby began, then stopped.

"What?" Jessica asked.

Abby shrugged. "Nothing." She had almost said it was funny that Jessica didn't know whether her dad was nice or not.

It wasn't really funny at all.

"I can't wait to meet Danielle and Dakota!" Jessica blurted out. "It's like having two instant sisters!"

"Add water and mix," Abby joked.

"One minute they're not there and then, pouf! They're here!" Jessica said. "It's like magic."

Abby nodded. "Now *you're* here, but in a week you won't be," she said. She still couldn't get used to the idea. And why hadn't Jessica said anything to her?

Jessica plunked herself down on Abby's bed. "What do you think it'll be like, Abby? Having sisters, I mean."

"Noisy," Abby said. She had a lot of experience with sisters.

"Don't you think it'll be wonderful?" Jessica sighed.

Abby made a face. "You can have the Twin Terrors anytime."

"I want sisters of my own," Jessica insisted.

Abby walked over to her desk and flipped open a calendar. "Aren't friends good enough?" she asked.

"You don't understand," Jessica said.

The two girls looked at each other. Abby caught her breath. There was so much more she wanted to say, but somehow she couldn't say a word.

Chapter 2

> **Friday**
>
> "The best of friends must part."

What my sister Isabel said after I hung up the phone with Jessica.

Why do the best of friends have to part???? I don't want to part from Jessica for three whole months!

She called while we were eating breakfast this morning to tell me that she's leaving on Sunday. That's only two days from now! That's five days earlier than she thought. She has to leave right away. That's <u>no fair</u>!

I'm not ready for Jessica to go so soon!

How Many Ways Will I Miss
My Best Friend?

1. No one to cheer me up when my SuperSibs argue and fight.

2. No one to talk to when everyone in my family is busy.

3. No one to explain the math problems I don't understand!

4. No one to laugh with when Brianna brags too much.

5. No one to have sleepovers with on weekends.

6. No one to −

Enough!!!! I can't think about any more ways I'll miss Jessica or I'll start crying right now.

My mother said three months isn't long. Before I know it, Jessica will be home again.

My mother is wrong! Three months is for-ever!!!!!!

Jessica called an emergency All-Friends meeting for lunch today. She, Natalie,

Sarah, and I will all sit together at the same lunch table.

I am so sad!

Will I be able to eat even a bite?

Notes to self:
1. Pack lunch I don't like. (I won't miss it if I'm too upset to eat.)
2. Bring container of sliced onions. (No one will wonder why I'm crying.)
3. Put tissues in lunch box instead of napkins.
4. Wear sunglasses to hide red eyes.

Today is the last day I will spend with Jessica for three months! Tomorrow she has to pack her suitcase and shop with her mother for holiday gifts.

On Sunday, she leaves.

My father said he'd take me to the air-port to say good-bye. (Thanks, Dad!) At least I'll be able to put it off until the very last minute.

"I can't believe you're going so soon!" Natalie wailed. "You'll miss the winter holidays and everything!"

"I'm not exactly missing them," Jessica pointed out. "I'll celebrate them with my father and his new family."

"But you won't be *here*," Abby said.

"No," Jessica agreed. She unwrapped a straw and poked it into her milk carton. "But I'll be *there*."

Sarah ran her fingers through her short, curly hair. "We won't be able to go skiing together during vacation."

"Or sledding," Abby said.

"Or show each other our presents," Natalie added.

The four fifth-grade girls sat at one end of the cafeteria table. Abby, Natalie, and Jessica were all in Ms. Kantor's class and had been good friends for a while. Sarah was in Mrs. McMillan's class. She and Jessica had recently become friends while working on a science fair project.

Natalie unwrapped a turkey sandwich, then put it down untouched. "I hate saying good-bye!"

"Me, too," Abby said. She wasn't *really* saying

good-bye now, since her dad was taking her to the airport. But she couldn't tell that to Natalie and Sarah. What if they wanted to come, too?

Abby wanted to be the last person to see Jessica. She was *her* best friend.

Jessica sighed. "I'm happy and I'm sad." She pushed away her milk carton. "I wish I could be in two places at once."

"What did Ms. Kantor say when you told her?" Sarah asked.

"She said she hoped I had a great visit with my dad," Jessica said, "and not to worry about missing anything."

"Gee, I wish she'd say that to me!" Natalie said.

"I wish she'd say that to me about math!" Abby said. "Even though I'm getting better at it."

"Do you think your new teacher will be as nice as Ms. Kantor?" Sarah asked Jessica.

"Danielle said she was," Jessica confided. "Her name is Ms. Allen. Danielle said Ms. Allen loves science."

"Just like you!" Sarah exclaimed.

"Will you have creative writing, too?" Natalie asked. "I bet you won't get a teacher like Ms. Bunder!"

"I don't know," Jessica said. "I hope there's a good art teacher, too."

Abby said nothing. She didn't want to think about Jessica in another classroom with new teachers and friends. She didn't want to think about her drawing funny pictures that Abby wouldn't see or helping someone else with her math problems. And who would Abby read her creative writing assignments to if Jessica wasn't there?

"Are you nervous about seeing your father again?" Natalie asked.

"We've talked on the phone a lot," Jessica said with a shrug. "And he's sent cards and presents. It's not like I don't know him."

Sarah nodded. "I bet you'll have a great time."

Jessica picked at a loose thread on her overalls. "There's just one thing I'm worried about," she began. "Not school, not home, not friends — "

"What else is there?" Abby interrupted.

"Work!" Jessica said. "I have dog-walking and baby-sitting jobs. I can't do them when I'm in Oregon."

"Unless you have a secret double," Abby said.

Sarah leaned forward. "*We* can help you!"

Abby wished that *she* had said it first. Then Jessica would be smiling at her instead of Sarah.

"Yes," Abby echoed. "I'll take over one of your jobs."

"Me, too," Natalie said.

"Really?" Jessica said. "Are you sure you want to?"

The four girls looked at each other.

"Why not?" Natalie said. "We'll earn money, won't we?"

Jessica nodded. "I have four dogs to walk every day after school. And baby-sitting three times a week. I earn twenty dollars a week for dog walking and eighteen to twenty-five dollars a week for baby-sitting."

"I'll dog walk!" Natalie and Sarah said at the same time.

"You can divide it up," Jessica suggested. "Each of you take two dogs. I'll set it up."

"I'll baby-sit," Abby offered. She was secretly relieved that Natalie and Sarah wanted to take over the dog walking. She had tried it before. Leashes got tangled; dogs chased anything that moved; and there were nasty messes to clean up.

Baby-sitting was much easier and much more fun.

"You'll be a mother's helper," Jessica explained. "Do you remember Geoffrey?"

Abby frowned. "The one who put maple syrup in your hair?"

"He's a lot better now," Jessica said quickly. "I've got him trained. I'll tell you everything before I go. Once you know the secret, it's easy."

"Good," Abby said.

"Don't worry," Natalie said to Jessica. "We'll take care of everything."

Jessica threw her arms around her friends. "You're all the greatest! I'll call Geoffrey's mom and the dog owners tonight and let them know."

As the girls walked slowly out of the cafeteria, Ms. Kantor hurried past them.

"The meeting starts in three minutes," she reminded them. "Hurry upstairs to the library!"

"We almost missed it!" Abby exclaimed. "All we've been thinking about is Jessica leaving!"

Ms. Kantor nodded. "I know you want to say good-bye, but we're counting on you! Don't forget that."

"Movie night?" Sarah asked.

"Yes," Natalie said.

A few days ago, the class had read about floods in another part of the country. They were planning a movie and popcorn night in the school gymnasium to raise money for families who had lost their homes. All the profits would be donated to a disaster relief fund.

"I'm doing publicity," Abby said. "I'm going to make posters and put them up in stores and schools."

"I'm on the cleanup committee," Jessica said. She made a face. "Or *was*. I won't be able to wash tables and throw away garbage if I'm in Oregon."

"You're going to miss all the fun!" Natalie joked.

"Are you on the cleanup committee, too?" Sarah asked.

"I'm on the committee that chooses the movie," Natalie replied. "We're also in charge of movie and equipment rental."

"Pick a sports film!" Sarah urged. "Or something with animals."

"I'm going to vote for a fantasy movie," Natalie said. "That's *my* favorite."

"What about a comedy?" Abby asked. "They're always popular."

"So are sad movies," Jessica pointed out.

The girls headed toward the library.

"Whatever happens, you have to let me know,"

Jessica said. "You're all going to e-mail me, aren't you?"

"Of course!" Abby promised.

"Sure," Sarah said.

"Yes," Natalie said.

Ms. Kantor waved the girls into the library. "Hurry up!" she called. "We're waiting for you!"

Sarah said good-bye and headed back downstairs. Abby, Jessica, and Natalie ran into the library.

Chapter 3

Sunday

"Out of sight, out of mind."

Telescope Calendar

Today Jessica gets on a plane. She is going to Oregon. She'll be out of sight, but she <u>won't</u> be out of mind.

I'll think about her all the time. I'll e-mail her every day.

I'll write her about movie night. I'll tell her my math quiz scores. I'll write about Geoffrey. (I hope there's not too much to tell!)

Almost New Year's Resolutions

1. Become a great baby-sitter.
2. Let Jessica know that her job is in good hands.

3. Make sure that she can come back and find everything the way it was.

4. Remind Jessica every day how much I miss her!!!

At the meeting on Friday, we tried to think of a name for our movie night fundraiser. Ms. Kantor kept asking me if I had any ideas. I didn't. She asked what was on my mind. I couldn't tell her. (Hint: It wasn't movie night.)

Fortunately, my classmates had lots of ideas.

Ms. Kantor's Fifth-Graders' Marvelous Movie Night Names

1. An Evening of Movies and Popcorn
2. Fabulous Food and Film Festival
3. The Silver Screen Savers
4. Munch and Watch
5. Lancaster Film Fair

And the winner is . . . The Silver Screen Savers. Do you think that's a

catchy name for the evening? I do! Here's
what I'm going to write on the poster:

THE SILVER SCREEN SAVERS
present a night of Family Fun,
Entertainment, and Refreshments.
   Relax, Watch a Movie, and Enjoy
Delicious Refreshments!

   Movie: TBA (To Be Announced)
   Date: Friday night
   Time: 7:00 P.M.
   Place: Lancaster Elementary
Cafeteria and Gymnasium
   Admission: $3.00 per person

   All profits will be donated to
charity!

 I'm going to write the names
of the refreshments up and
down the sides of the poster.
Popcorn! Brownies! Cider!

Muffins! There will be pictures, too.

I hope we offer popcorn, brownies, and cider. Brianna is on the refreshment committee, and she has other ideas.

Refreshments Brianna Wants to Serve

Petit fours (huh?), cheesecake cookies (really?), and glazed chocolate almond crescents (huh? again)

Mulled cider, sparkling grape juice, mango punch

Refreshments the Other Kids on the Committee Want to Serve

Popcorn, brownies, vanilla cupcakes, and donuts (hooray!)

Cider, hot chocolate, and orange juice

Number of Other Kids on the Committee

Four

Number of Briannas on the Committee

One

Reason We Might All Eat Petits Fours on Movie Night Instead of Donuts

No one wants to argue with Brianna!

Question: What is a petit four? And why _does_ Brianna want us to eat them instead of brownies?

When we decide on refreshments and the movie, I'm going to print out a poster, make hundreds of copies, and put them up in supermarkets, restaurants, bookstores, and schools. I will call the local radio and TV stations and ask them to make announcements. Hundreds of people will show up for the Silver Screen Savers movie night. Ms. Kantor's class will make buckets of money for the families who lost their homes!

What color paper shall I print out the posters on? Electric blue? Lime green? Bright yellow? Vivid orange? Wild purple? One of them or all of them?
What font will I use?
What does a petit four look like?

Should I sign each poster "An Abby Hayes Original!"?

INTERRUPTION!!!
Dad just told me to get ready. It's time to go to the airport. I've been trying not to think about it.

BOOHOO!!!!

"Parting is such sweet sorrow."
William Shakespeare said that. So did Isabel this morning at breakfast.
Why is parting "sweet"? I don't think so! It is painful, agonizing, sad, desperate, unhappy, and miserable. There is nothing sweet about it!

Dad just knocked on my door. I have to go.

<u>A Heartrending Tale of Incredible Tragedy</u>
by Abby Hayes

It was a dark and stormy night.

No, it wasn't.

Actually, it was a sunny and pleasant morning. But it <u>should</u> have been a dark and stormy night.

Paul Hayes and Abby Hayes got into the minivan. Paul Hayes put the key in the ignition.

"Wait a minute," he said to his daughter. "I forgot my coffee."

"Dad!" Abby cried. "I don't want to miss saying good-bye to Jessica!"

"Don't worry," Paul Hayes said. He ran back into the house. A minute later, he came back with a thermos filled with coffee. He was whistling.

"Remind me to buy bagels on the way home," he said as they pulled out of the driveway.

"Bagels?"

"Onion, sesame, and cinnamon raisin," her father said. "And a tub of cream cheese, too."

Abby sighed. This was one of the saddest moments of her life, and her father was talking about breakfast.

At the airport, Abby and her father

walked to the gate to find Jessica and her mother. As they approached the waiting area, Abby suddenly wanted to turn around and run. Maybe if she didn't say good-bye, Jessica wouldn't leave.

Her father touched her arm. "You okay?"

Abby nodded.

Jessica was looking out the window at the tarmac. She was wearing overalls, a striped sweater, and sneakers, and she carried a backpack and a book. She was watching baggage handlers load suitcases onto the plane. She looked happier than Abby expected.

Her mother stood next to her, with a worried frown on her face.

"You know what happens when you get to Chicago?" her mother asked.

"Yes, Mom," Jessica began. She turned around suddenly.

"Abby! You're here!" she cried.

Abby tried to smile. She couldn't say anything.

Jessica's mother greeted Abby and her father. "Thanks for coming," she said. "We're happy you came to see Jessica off."

"I brought this for you." Abby thrust a paper bag into Jessica's hand.

Jessica's eyes lit up. "Can I open it now?"

"Sure. Why not?"

"Don't leave us in suspense, Jessica," Paul Hayes said.

Jessica pulled out a giant chocolate bar with almonds. It was her favorite kind.

"It's for the plane," Abby said. "In case you get hungry."

The next present was a bright turquoise journal with a package of gel pens taped to its cover.

"Just what you need," Jessica's mother commented. "Now you can write down everything that happens to you."

"Thanks!" Jessica said. "I love it!"

"There's more," Abby said.

"More?" Jessica repeated. She pulled out a calendar. On the cover was a photo of Abby and Jessica on Rollerblades. The name of the calendar was printed in large purple letters: OREGON ADVENTURES.

"I made it on the computer," Abby explained. "It's a three-month calendar for your visit. Look inside."

Jessica flipped through the calendar. Each page had pictures of Abby and Jessica, from kindergarten through fifth grade. The days of the week were decorated with soccer balls, rainbows, and butterflies.

"You even put quotes for every month!" Jessica cried. "This is the greatest!"

"And that's not all," Paul Hayes said, handing her a small package with a blue bow. "This is from the rest of the Hayes family."

"A disposable camera!" Jessica exclaimed.

"We hope you have a fine visit with your father and his family," Paul Hayes said, "and bring us back a snapshot or two."

"Don't take pictures of people's ankles, like Alex does," Abby warned her.

Jessica hugged Abby. "You're the best friend in the world!"

"I hope you like Danielle and Dakota," Abby said. "But not better than any of the friends you have here!"

"Our flight is now boarding," a crew member announced. "Those sitting in rows thirty-six to twenty-four, those requiring assistance, and families with young children may now begin to board."

Jessica examined her ticket. "I'm in row eleven," she said. "I don't board yet." She put the presents into her backpack.

"Remember, the airline will send an escort to meet you in Chicago," her mother began.

Jessica clapped her hand to her forehead. "I forgot!"

Her mother frowned. "The escort? Jessica, you can't forget!"

"Not that." Jessica turned to Abby. "I forgot to tell you the secret."

"Rows twenty-four to twelve may now board," the announcer intoned.

"The secret?" Abby asked.

It sounded like a mystery novel. Did Jessica know where treasure was buried?

What problems were going to be on the next math test? Whom Brianna had a crush on?

"Of how to handle Geoffrey," Jessica explained.

"Geoffrey!" Abby exclaimed. "Oh, no!" Jessica had told her all about his pranks and mischief. She didn't want to show up without a plan. It was her key to success.

"Don't worry," Jessica said. "I know how to deal with Geoffrey. You have to –"

"All remaining passengers may now board the plane."

"What's the secret?" Abby cried.

"I'll e-mail you!" Jessica promised. She kissed her mother good-bye and handed the flight attendant her ticket.

"Don't forget!" Abby called. "I'm watching him on Tuesday!"

Jessica waved one last time and disappeared down the ramp.

Chapter 4

Tuesday

"No man's knowledge here can go beyond his experience."
—*John Locke*

1001 Things to Do with String Calendar

Whoever wrote that quote never had a best friend. (Or does the quote only apply to "man" and not "girl"?)

My knowledge of Geoffrey <u>does</u> go beyond my experience.

That's because Jessica e-mailed me her top secret tips on how to deal with him.

<u>Jessica's Best Geoffrey-Taming Tips</u>

1. When he starts having tantrums, read him <u>Itty Baby in the Bath</u>.

2. If he says no to every-thing, get out his dump truck.

3. When all else fails, give him chocolate pudding.

It's easy! Anyone can do it! Thanks to Jessica's experience, I have all the knowledge I need.

I will keep her job ready for her.

When she comes home, it'll be as if she never left.

She'll be <u>so</u> grateful and happy!

Our friendship will be good, better, best, <u>bester</u>!!! (Is "bester" a word? It should be!)

"Wish me luck," Abby said as she and Natalie walked home from school together. "I'm going to Geoffrey's house for my first day of baby-sitting."

Natalie raised her eyebrows. "You need more than luck with Geoffrey. I watched him once. He's a terror."

"Jessica said you just have to know how to handle him."

"Really?" Natalie didn't sound convinced. "I'm glad *I'm* dog walking." She glanced at her watch. "Half an hour until I start. I can't wait!"

"I have all of Jessica's baby-sitting tips right here.

With her advice, I can't fail," Abby insisted, pulling a crumpled sheet of paper from her pocket. "See?"

Natalie glanced briefly at the paper and shrugged. "How's Jessica?" she asked.

"She has to share a room with Danielle. She said the room is really messy."

"I bet Jessica hates that!"

All her friends knew that Jessica was a neat freak. Clothes were always folded or hung in the closet. Papers were organized in folders. The bed was always made.

"And Danielle likes to dress up and go to parties," Abby said. "She has millions of friends."

"She sounds like Jessica's opposite," Natalie commented.

"I hope Danielle isn't like Brianna," Abby said.

Natalie made a face. "Did you hear her today?" She flipped an imaginary mane of hair over her shoulder in imitation of Brianna.

"Brownies and donuts are boring!" she proclaimed in a Brianna-like voice. "*My* committee will serve only the best and most original pastries."

"My brownies are all Broadway stars," Abby mimicked. "My donuts speak French."

"And my cider wears the coolest clothes," Natalie finished.

The two girls began to laugh.

"Good thing Victoria isn't on the refreshment committee, too," Abby said, referring to Brianna's best friend. "Or on the movie committee!"

Natalie shuddered. "She'd make us watch Tiffany Crystal videos!"

"*Ugh!*" Abby cried.

"We're arguing about the movies anyway," Natalie said. "Most of the kids on my committee want to see *Twenty-two Rottweilers*."

"That movie about the family who adopted all the dogs?" Abby asked. "Everyone's seen it a million times!"

"I know!" Natalie said. "The other movie everyone wants is *The Princess Mermaid*."

"I *hate* that movie!" Abby said.

"No one can agree on a fantasy movie," Natalie said glumly. "Most of them aren't that good. The books are usually better."

"Ms. Bunder says magic takes place in your mind," Abby said. Ms. Bunder was the creative writing teacher. Creative writing was Abby's favorite subject.

"I wish the magic took place on-screen," Natalie said. "Where is the movie that *everyone* wants to see? We have to find it!"

"Yeah," Abby agreed. "Until you decide, I can't make the posters. If I don't put the posters up, no one will know about the event."

Natalie stopped. "There's Geoffrey's house."

The two-story house was painted pale blue with white trim. Neatly pruned bushes lined the yard. There was a tricycle overturned on the sidewalk.

"It's like every other house on the block," Abby said.

"But it has Geoffrey inside," Natalie warned her. "I'd rather walk a hundred dogs together than baby-sit one of him."

"He can't be that bad," Abby said. She patted her pocket. "Besides, I've got all of Jessica's secrets right here."

Natalie looked doubtful. "Well . . . good luck!" she finally said, checking her watch. "It's time for me to walk the dogs! *Hooray!!!*"

She said good-bye and hurried down the block.

Abby pulled out Jessica's e-mail and studied it one last time.

"Don't get scared by his temper tantrums," Jessica

had written. "Remain calm, find his favorite book, and start reading it."

"Okay, I will," Abby said.

Jessica's tips would make all the difference in taking care of Geoffrey. And Abby would make sure that she took care of Jessica's job.

She took a deep breath, went up the stairs, and rang the doorbell.

"You must be Abby. I'm Elaine, Geoffrey's mom." The woman who opened the door was wearing blue jeans and a sweater. She had a friendly smile. "Come in. Geoffrey is so excited that you'll be playing with him."

"Hi," Abby said. "Nice to meet you." She stepped into the hallway. There were clothes and toys scattered on the floor.

"Excuse the mess," Elaine said, running her hands through her hair.

She led Abby into a living room even messier than the hallway. "Geoffrey!" she called. "Abby's here!"

There was no answer.

"Geoffrey?!"

"BOO!" Geoffrey yelled, jumping out from behind the couch.

He was small and blond. There was a large smear of jam on his face.

"Hi, Geoffrey," Abby said. She smiled at him. "I'm Abby."

Geoffrey stared at her. He twisted his face into a terrible grimace. Then he ran to his mother and flung his arms around her legs.

"Abby is Jessica's friend," Elaine said. "She's going to play with you today."

"No!" Geoffrey said.

"Mommy has to work. Don't you want to show Abby all your toys?"

"No!" Geoffrey said.

Abby got down on her knees and picked up a fire truck. "Vroom! Vroom! Vroom!"

"You can show Abby where everything is," Elaine said. "She'll give you your favorite snack."

"Chocolate pudding," Abby said.

From behind his mother's legs, Geoffrey watched her. "I want to play with my walkie-talkie."

"Okay," Abby said. "Where is it?"

He scampered into the next room.

Elaine smiled at her. "You're going to do fine. My office is upstairs, over the garage. If you need me, come get me."

She disappeared out the back door. Geoffrey ran into the room with two walkie-talkies in his hand.

"Where's Mommy?" he demanded. "Where'd she go?"

"She's working," Abby said.

"Mommy! I want Mommy! I want her now!"

Geoffrey's voice rose in pitch.

Abby pointed to the walkie-talkies. "Don't you want to play with them?"

"Mommy! Mommy!" Geoffrey yelled.

Abby's heart raced. How had Jessica done it? She didn't have a clue what to do next.

"You can be a policeman," she said. "Or do you want to be a pilot?"

Suddenly Geoffrey stopped yelling. He handed her a walkie-talkie.

Abby breathed a sigh of relief.

"You stay here," he ordered. "I'll hide. Then I'll call you."

"Okay," Abby agreed. She sat down on the couch and waited.

Chapter 5

Tuesday

"Silence is golden."
Bells and Chimes Calendar

Silence is also scary, ominous, unpleasant, disturbing, upsetting, frightening, and alarming.

Especially when you're baby-sitting Geoffrey.

Especially when you don't know where he is.

Especially when you don't know where to look.

Especially when the silence goes on and on and on and on. . . .

Where is he???

One after another, Abby pushed the buttons on the walkie-talkie. "Geoffrey?" she said. "*Geoffrey?*"

There was no answer.

Abby unfolded her copy of Jessica's e-mail and scanned it quickly. Jessica had not sent her any tips on what to do if Geoffrey disappeared.

What would Jessica do in her place? Jessica always knew exactly what to do. So why didn't Abby?

"Geoffrey!!" Abby called. "Geoffrey!!!"

Abby ran from room to room, calling his name.

No Geoffrey in sight.

He wasn't in the kitchen, the dining room, or the downstairs bathroom.

Frantically she dashed upstairs. She flung open doors, peered under beds, and checked closets and shower stalls.

She ran back downstairs. Her heart was racing. What if he had gone outside? What if he had gone to a neighbor's house? What if he was already someplace she couldn't find him?

If she couldn't find Geoffrey, she'd have to find Elaine. Elaine would fire her. Abby would have to write to Jessica and admit that she'd failed to keep her job. She would have let her best friend down when Jessica needed her most.

"BOO!" Geoffrey jumped out from behind the door and made a horrible face at Abby.

Abby collapsed on the couch.

"I want chocolate pudding! Now!"

"Wait." Abby held up her hand. She had to catch her breath. She felt like she had just done the hundred-yard dash.

"Were you hiding behind the door all the time?"

Geoffrey nodded.

"Did you hear me calling you?"

He nodded again.

"Why didn't you answer?"

Geoffrey made another horrible face.

"Is that all you have to say?"

"Blub."

Abby stood up. "It's time for chocolate pudding," she said.

She marched into the kitchen, keeping a close eye on Geoffrey. She didn't think he'd hide again if chocolate pudding was in sight, but she didn't trust him for a second.

*　*　*

"Thanks again," Elaine said. She handed Abby a five- and a one-dollar bill. "You did a good job."

"Uh, thanks." Abby glanced at Geoffrey. He was hanging on to his mother's legs. There was chocolate pudding all over his shirt.

"We'll see you Thursday?"

"Uh, yeah," Abby said, putting the money in her jeans pocket. "Good-bye, Geoffrey."

"No!" Geoffrey said.

Abby waved to Elaine and ran down the porch steps. The cold air was refreshing on her face. She couldn't wait to get home.

Somehow she had made it through an afternoon with Geoffrey. He'd had only two tantrums, hidden for a mere twenty minutes, and dumped chocolate pudding in her lap only once. After cleaning up the chocolate pudding, she had read his favorite book, *Itty Baby in the Bath*, at least two hundred times.

Now she could recite it by heart, along with Geoffrey:

*"Itty Baby in the Bath
Likes to Swim
And do his Math . . .*

One, Two, Three, Four,
Itty Baby, count some more!"

"One, two, three, four," Abby recited as she hurried home. "I can't stand Itty Baby anymore!"

Yes, she had gotten through one afternoon. But then there was Thursday . . . and Saturday morning . . . and next Tuesday . . . and the Thursday after. . . .

How had Jessica done it????

She must have Super Sitter powers and chocolate-proof clothes. She could stop terrible tantrums in the blink of an eye. She could leap over couches and see behind doors to find the most well-hidden toddler!

If Jessica were home, Abby would be on the phone with her right now. She would be confiding every detail of her afternoon with Geoffrey. They would be laughing about it together and figuring out what to do next. But Jessica was in Oregon. She wasn't easy to reach.

Why did Jessica have to leave??

"Hey, Hayes! Howdy!"

Only one person in Lancaster Elementary called Abby "Hayes." And only one person would think it was funny to say "howdy."

"Hi, Hoffman," Abby retorted. It wasn't much of

a retort, but after reading *Itty Baby in the Bath* all afternoon, it was the best she could do.

Casey Hoffman was Abby's only friend who was a boy. But he was NOT a boyfriend. (No matter what Brianna said.)

"Urp!" Mason announced his presence with a belch.

Mason was big, bold, and boisterous. He was the one boy Brianna couldn't stand.

"The Big Burper is here," Casey said.

Both boys had rakes in their hands.

"Casey and I have earned fifteen dollars this afternoon," Mason bragged. "That's seven-fifty apiece."

"Plus cookies and apple cider," Casey added. "Do you want to join us raking leaves, Hayes?"

"Leaves, Hayes?" Mason repeated, punctuating his comment with another loud burp. "How about raking Hayes, leaves?"

"That doesn't make any sense," Abby said.

"No," Casey agreed. "Try again, Mason." He winked at Abby.

"Eeerp!" Mason said instead.

"I just earned six dollars," Abby said. "Plus chocolate pudding." She was glad her coat was long. It covered the stains.

"What were you doing?" Casey asked.

"Baby-sitting." Abby pointed to Geoffrey's house. "It's Jessica's job."

"I know that Geoffrey kid," Mason said. "My sister Kathleen baby-sits him on Saturday nights."

"Really?" Abby said. "Does she like him?"

Mason shrugged. "She says he's cute."

"Cute?" Abby repeated. "That's not how — " She stopped. Maybe Kathleen knew how to handle Geoffrey. After all, Mason was her brother.

Once again she wished that Jessica wasn't so far away.

The streetlights flickered and came on.

Casey checked his watch. "I'm late," he said. "My parents don't like me to be out after dark."

"Me, neither," Abby said. She glanced at the sky. "It's not dark yet, but it will be soon."

"We'll walk home together," Casey offered.

Mason brandished his rake. "If anyone tries to bother us . . ."

"You'll burp," Abby finished.

"He's trained himself carefully," Casey told Abby. "Long, lonely years were spent developing his special talent. Now he's the only kid in the fifth grade who can burp on demand."

"Even Brianna is jealous!" Mason cackled.

"Yeah, right," Abby said.

The three fifth-graders walked home under the streetlamps. Newly fallen leaves crackled under their feet. The sidewalk in front of Abby's house was covered with them.

"See you tomorrow in school," Abby said.

"See tomorrow in school, you!" Casey replied.

"Not funny, Hoffman!" Mason slapped him on the back.

"Good-bye!" Abby yelled as she ran up the driveway. It was fun to see Casey and Mason outside of school. But they still weren't Jessica.

Abby rushed into the house. "I'm home!" she called. "I'm back!"

"How did it go?" her mother asked. She was still in her work clothes but wore fuzzy slippers on her feet.

"Well," Abby began. She was dying to tell *someone* about her afternoon.

"Mom!!! Where's my basketball jersey?" Eva demanded, rushing into the room. "I have practice in fifteen minutes!"

"Sorry, Abby. Later," her mother said.

Abby took off her coat and boots and went into the kitchen. "I'm back from my baby-sitting job," she announced.

"Congratulations," her father said. He stirred a pot of tomato sauce. "I hope you didn't walk home alone in the dark."

"I walked home with Mason and Casey. They were raking lawns."

"While they were walking home?" her father teased.

"Dad!" Abby protested.

Her father smiled.

"Aren't you going to ask me how it went?" Abby said.

"How what went?"

"Baby-sitting Geoffrey!!"

Her father gave her a hug. "I'm sure you were wonderful."

"Well," Abby began again. Her father was the perfect person to talk to. He'd have something funny to say and then he'd offer sensible advice. He was almost as good as Jessica.

She took a breath. "Geof — "

Isabel stormed into the kitchen. "Terrible news! I placed third in the history competition. *Third!*"

"Sounds good to me," her father commented. "Especially statewide."

"But I should have been first!" Isabel exclaimed.

"Geoffrey dumped chocolate pudding on my la — " Abby said.

"Abby! This is no time to talk about chocolate pudding!" Isabel cried.

"But Geoffrey — " Abby protested.

"Never mind Geoffrey! This is a tragedy!" Isabel proclaimed, tossing her head dramatically.

Paul Hayes glanced at Abby. "Sorry, honey," he said. "Why don't you tell me all about it later?"

Why did Jessica have to go to Oregon?

Abby wandered into Alex's room. He was reading a book.

"Do you want to hear about my baby-sitting job?" she asked.

He didn't answer.

"I didn't think so," Abby said.

Chapter 6

Tuesday

"Everything's relative."

Kinship Calendar

I wish it wasn't! Then it wouldn't bother me so much when my relatives don't have time for me.

<u>Everything's Relative, or Abby's Brief Theory of Relativity</u>

1. Usually I hate homework. After babysitting Geoffrey, it's a relief to do homework. (Homework doesn't hide. Or throw chocolate pudding. Or do anything unexpected.)

2. Jessica is far away. When my whole family is too busy to talk to me, she's the closest person around.

Relatively Important Questions

1. How do you get chocolate pudding stains out of clothes?

2. How many times can a person read Itty Baby in the Bath without going insane?

3. Is Mason really as obnoxious as he seems? (Or is he secretly nice?)

4. Why does everyone in my family keep saying, "Sorry, Abby. Later"?

5. When will Jessica answer my e-mail? It's two days since I wrote her. I need more Geoffrey-taming tips! I want to know what she's doing! I need to know if she misses me as much as I miss her!

Wednesday

Still no answer from Jessica. What's happened to her????

a) She is so happy that she's forgotten all about us!

b) She's so unhappy that she's forgotten all about us!

c) She's forgotten all about us! (Out of sight, out of mind? Nooooooo . . .)

My gloomy thoughts are interrupted by a call from Natalie.

Hooray! I can talk to Natalie! She will sympathize with my terrible ordeal.

A Conversation Between Two Friends

Natalie: The movie committee is going to make their decision soon. But first we're polling class members. Do you think we should see <u>Twenty-two Rottweilers</u>? Or <u>The Princess Mermaid</u>? Or <u>Asteroid!</u>? Or <u>The Tiffany Crystal Story</u>?

Abby (dismayed): Those are the choices?

Natalie: Unless you want to see <u>The Aardvark King</u>.

Abby: Ugh.

Natalie: I agree.

Abby: What about <u>Darling, I've Shrink-wrapped My Elbow</u>?

Natalie: No one likes that one.

Abby (desperate): <u>Bub</u>?

Natalie: Are you serious?

Abby: No.

Natalie: Well, what's your choice?

Abby: <u>Secret of the Baby-sitters, Part II</u>.

Natalie: That's a good one. Why don't you come to the meeting tomorrow after school and suggest it?

Abby: I have to watch Geoffrey.

Natalie: Too bad.

Abby: That's for sure.

Natalie: Huh?

Abby (hopeful): It's a long story. Do you want to hear it?

Natalie: Later. I still have half the class to call.

Abby: Never mind. Which movie do you think will win?

Natalie: <u>The Princess Mermaid</u>.

Abby: Does that mean mermaids on the poster?

Natalie: Yes.

Abby: I guess they're better than aardvarks – or Tiffany Crystal.

After I hung up the phone, I checked

my e-mail again. Still nothing from Jessica. Went to find T-Jeff. He was sleeping in the upstairs closet. I petted him until he started to purr.

T-Jeff, you're always my friend! Even when no one else is around.

Thursday noon

Natalie and Sarah and Bethany and I had lunch together.

They asked me if I'd heard from Jessica. I asked them if they had heard from her. None of us had.

What We Talked About

Sarah: Skiing. Now that Jessica is gone, she's looking for another friend to ski with.

Natalie: Movies. Says it's too bad Jessica can't vote for her favorite movie.

Bethany: Pets. Wonders if Dakota and Danielle have any.

Abby: Nothing.

What We Didn't Talk About

Why it isn't any fun to eat lunch to-gether now that Jessica is gone.

Why everyone always talks about the same thing, over and over.

They argued about movies for the rest of lunch period. I pretended to listen but was really thinking about Jessica.

And Geoffrey, of course. I have to baby-sit him in only a few short hours. I asked Sarah, Natalie, and Bethany for advice. They didn't have anything to say.

Jessica _always_ has advice!

Thursday, 3:00 P.M.

Why does school have to end?

Thursday, 3:05 P.M.

Off to meet my doom! Into the House of Geoffrey. (Good subject for horror movie. Be sure to suggest it for movie night.)

I have to baby-sit <u>again</u> on Saturday. How did Jessica do it? (She dog walked, too!)

<u>Scene</u>
The fearless fifth-grader with curly red hair puts on her pea coat. With a careless nod to her friends, she winds her striped scarf around her neck. Bravely, she shoulders her backpack.

"Good luck!" Natalie and Bethany call to her. They leave the classroom together, chatting, ignorant of the dangers that their close friend will soon encounter.

Abby walks out of the school alone. She faces into the wind, which is brisk and cold.

"Eeerp!" Mason comes up behind her and tries to startle her.

"Oh, hi, Mason," Abby says. Even world-class burps can't upset her now, when she is on her way to Geoffrey's house.

"Walking this way?" Mason asks.

"Uh-huh," Abby answers. She is deep in thought. She is trying to think of what to do over the next three hours. Dance? Sing? Stand on her head?

She is facing a doom darker and stickier than any known to man, woman, or child.

Suddenly she remembers. Mason's sister has taken care of Geoffrey. "Is Kathleen home?" she asks the Big Burper.

"No," Mason says.

Her last hopes are dashed. Geoffrey's house looms on the corner. The windows gleam with an evil light. . . .

Thursday, 6:35 P.M.

I am still alive!!!!

Not only that, but baby-sitting Geoffrey was okay . . . ???
Can it be true?

Did we really go to the park and have fun on the swings?

Did I only have to read his favorite book three times?

Did he really sulk when I left?

1. Pinch arm to see if dreaming.
2. Call Natalie to announce news. (It doesn't matter if she's not home!)
3. Breathe GIGANTIC sigh of relief!

Am I a natural baby-sitter? Or even a baby-sitting genius, like Jessica? Maybe I'm a Super Sitter, too!

Ha-ha-ha! I did it all myself, without any help from anyone! And I have twelve dollars in my pocket to spend any way I please!

HOORAY!!!

I am saving Jessica's job for her. Can I do it again? And again and again and again?

I <u>have</u> to keep this up.

I must, I must, I must!

(Otherwise, I'm going to need someone to save <u>me</u> from Jessica's job!)

Chapter 7

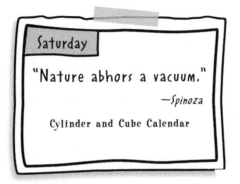

Saturday

"Nature abhors a vacuum."
—*Spinoza*

Cylinder and Cube Calendar

Does Nature also abhor vacuum cleaners? I do! (Abhor means hate. Thank you, Isabel Hayes, human dictionary.)

I also abhor dust rags, brooms, and ammonia!

In addition, I abhor cleaning my room, especially early on a Saturday morning.

<u>Saturdays should be dedicated to fun!!!!</u>

No responsibilities of any kind. No house-work. And no thinking about school — not even about movie night.

(What would my parents say about No Responsibility Saturdays? I don't think they'd agree!)

I don't abhor writing in my journal. Or seeing my friends. Or e-mailing them. Jessica finally e-mailed me! She apologized for not answering me sooner.

Geoffrey tests his baby-sitters, she wrote. I hope I passed. I don't want to take the test again.

Jessica is swimming almost every night with Danielle. They have more homework than we do. She sounded really busy. But she said she misses us!

I still miss her, too.

But I can't sit around the house feeling sad and lonely. Three months is a long time. Jessica is having fun with Danielle. I'll have fun with other friends, too! Maybe I'll even make new friends!

Abby gave her bureau a final swipe with the dust rag, sneezed once, and sat down on her bed. The room smelled of lemon polish. The sun shone through the freshly cleaned window.

As Abby stared at the bright purple walls and the calendars that covered them, a knock sounded on her door.

"Abby!" Eva called. "Phone for you."

Abby wiped her hands on her jeans and took the phone. "Hello?"

"Hey, Hayes," Casey said.

"Hi, Hoffman?" Abby replied, in surprise. Casey didn't often call her. "What's up?"

"I have an extra ticket for a college soccer game today. Want to come?"

"Soccer? I love soccer," Abby said.

"It's going to be an exciting match," Casey promised.

"Great! I'll ask my parents. Hold on."

Just a few minutes ago, she had been writing in her journal about doing new things with new people. Here was her chance.

Abby put down the phone and went to look for her mom and dad. She hoped they would say yes. She really wanted to go.

"Dad?" she called. She ran up the stairs to her father's home office. No one was there.

"Eva?" Abby banged at her door. "Where are Mom and Dad?"

Her older sister was doing sit-ups. "I dunno. Somewhere."

Abby ran downstairs.

At the kitchen table, Isabel sat in front of a pile of books. She was taking notes on a laptop computer.

"Where are Mom and Dad?" Abby asked.

"Out," Isabel said vaguely.

"Will they be back soon?"

"I hope so." Isabel tapped a quick sentence onto the screen.

"Casey invited me to a soccer game." Abby frowned at her sister. "Do you think it's okay if I go? I finished cleaning my room."

Isabel looked up from the computer. "Did you do all your homework?"

"I don't have any," Abby said.

"Wait until you get to high school," Isabel promised. "You'll have *hours* of it!"

"Did Mom and Dad leave you in charge?" Abby asked. "Or Eva?"

"Me, of course," Isabel said.

"I have basketball practice." Eva had a gym bag slung over her shoulder. "Otherwise *I'd* be in charge."

Opening the back door, Eva let in a blast of icy air. She smirked at her twin and slammed the door shut.

"Well, what do you think?" Abby demanded. She knew better than to take sides in any argument between her sisters. "Can I go? Casey's waiting."

"Leave a note for Mom and Dad," Isabel said, returning to her work. "Tell them where you are, who you're with, when you'll be back. They know Casey's parents. It should be fine."

"Yay!" Abby cried.

She went back upstairs and picked up the phone. "I can go!" she cried.

Casey sounded pleased. "We'll pick you up in half an hour. Mason's mother is driving."

"Mason's mother?" Abby didn't know her — and neither did her parents. She wondered what they would say. She hoped it would be okay.

"Is Mason coming, too?"

"The Big Burper gave me the tickets," Casey said.

"You sit between us," Abby instructed him.

Abby opened the back door of the car. Casey was sitting next to the window. In the front sat Mason and his mother.

"Hello, I'm Betsy," Mason's mother said. She was a large woman with a booming voice. "Are you Abby?"

"Uh-huh," Abby said. She slid into the seat next to Casey. "Nice to meet you."

"Don't say that!" Betsy warned, adjusting the headset of her cell phone. "It might not be nice to meet me."

"Yes, it is!" Casey protested.

"Uurrrp," Mason said.

"I knew you were going to say that," Abby said.

"He's so predictable," Betsy said. The cell phone rang. The ringer had been set to play "Happy Birthday."

"Hello? Hello?" Betsy said. She punched some buttons, then sighed. "Hung up. Wrong number."

"Is it someone's birthday?" Abby asked.

"Nope," Betsy said cheerfully. "I just like the tune." She fiddled with the radio dial. "What kind of music do you like, Abby? Country and western? Oldies? Tiffany Crystal? Opera?"

It was exciting to be on her way to a soccer match with different friends, Abby thought. She enjoyed being with boys for a change. And meeting Mason's mom, too.

"I like the Bumble Boys," Abby said to Betsy.

"They're the worst!" Mason cried.

"Thank you for making my son speak," Betsy said

to Abby. "I thought we were in the middle of a record-breaking burp-a-thon."

The cell phone rang again. The happy birthday tune jingled.

"Hello?" Betsy yelled. "Was that just you?"

In the backseat, Abby and Casey exchanged grins.

"Mason, I'll put you in *The Hayes Book of World Records* for Biggest and Best Burping," Abby offered. "You'll get your own page."

"Oh, wow," Mason said, punctuating his comment with yet another burp.

"That wasn't Biggest and Best," Betsy complained, switching off the phone. "Don't disappoint your friends."

"We're not disappointed!" Abby cried.

"Hayes speaks for us all," Casey said.

Betsy turned into a parking lot. "We're here because we're here because we're . . ."

The phone rang again.

"Enough is enough," Betsy announced.

"Eerp!" Mason said.

The fifth-graders piled out of the car.

"Go right over there!" Betsy ordered them. "Show your tickets, and get good seats! That's a command!"

Abby followed Mason. She was having more fun

than she had had in a while. Maybe it was even better than *before* Jessica had left.

Mason handed over the tickets and the three fifth-graders climbed into the bleachers together.

As they left the stadium a few hours later, a brisk wind blew up. Abby wound her scarf more tightly around her neck. She was glad she had worn her winter coat and gloves.

"Wasn't that a great game, Hayes?" Casey said.

"I loved it," she replied. "It was exciting when they scored the winning goal at the last minute!"

"The goalie just missed the ball," Mason said. "His teammates must be mad at him!"

"There's your mother," Abby said, pointing to Betsy. She stood in front of her car, gesturing to the fifth-graders.

"Hurry up!" she yelled. "It's freezing!"

As they dashed toward the car, brightly colored leaves fluttered to the ground.

"It's leaf-raking weather," Casey commented. "We have twelve jobs lined up for next week. More than the two of us can rake."

"We're going to make a pile of money!" Mason said gleefully. "Enough to jump in!"

"Well, I made twelve dollars last week," Abby bragged. "Just from baby-sitting Geof — "

She stopped suddenly.

Mason opened the car door for his friends. "Get in!"

They piled into the car.

"How was the game?" Betsy asked in a loud, cheerful voice.

"Awesome," Mason said, punching the air.

"Awfully awesome," Casey added. "Amazingly awesome! Agree, Abby?"

Abby shook her head. Even though Casey had called her Abby for the first time in history, she still couldn't say a word.

"What's the matter?" Betsy frowned. She turned the key in the ignition.

"Is the goalie your brother?" Mason asked.

Abby pointed to Casey's watch.

"It's one o'clock," Casey said. "Are you okay, Hayes?"

"No," Abby whispered. "I'm not. I was supposed to baby-sit Geoffrey at ten o'clock this morning. I forgot all about it."

Chapter 8

Saturday afternoon

"And we forget because we must and not because we will."

—*Matthew Arnold*
Responsible Reminder Calendar

<u>Must</u> I have forgotten about baby-sitting Geoffrey this morning?

1. I wrote down the date on five different calendars. (But I forgot to check them.)

2. Isabel asked me if I was done with my work. I said yes. (But I forgot about baby-sitting work.)

3. Mom and Dad might have reminded me about it. (But they weren't here.)

<u>Conclusion</u>

I didn't want to forget! (But I did!)

Painful Questions

Did I forget because I needed to have fun with Mason and Casey?

Did I forget because I _did_ have fun with Mason and Casey? (And Betsy, too.)

More Painful Questions

What will happen when I get home? What will Elaine say? What will Mom and Dad say? What will Jessica say? What will _I_ say?

Jessica will be _so_ angry! She never forgets anything. She's always responsible, always on time, and always organized.

She won't understand how I forgot about Geoffrey.

Why does my best friend have to be per- fect . . . like the rest of my family!!!

Abby climbed out of the car.

"Thanks for the ride," she said to Betsy. "Thanks for inviting me," she said to Mason and Casey.

"Good luck," Betsy said. "We all make mistakes."

Abby took a deep breath. She didn't think her parents would say that. Both cars were in the garage. She wondered if Elaine had called and talked to them.

"Don't worry, Hayes," Casey said.

"Eeerp," Mason added. "Just trying to cheer you up," he explained.

Abby waved good-bye and walked slowly up the driveway.

The front door opened. It was Alex. His hair stuck straight up, as if he had glued it.

"Abby!" he said. "Jessica called from Oregon!"

"Jessica!!!???" Abby cried. "Did you talk to her? How is she? What did she say?"

"She said hi," Alex said.

"That's *it*? Hi?"

"And don't call her; she's going ice-skating with Danielle."

"Oh." Disappointed, Abby shut the front door behind her. She hung her coat in the closet and kicked off her boots. "Will she call me back?"

"If she has time," Alex said. He picked up the cordless phone. "Peter's going to call me soon."

"Sure," Abby said. She walked into the living room. "Anyone else call?"

Alex shrugged. "Ask Mom."

She sat down on the couch. Maybe it was just as well that she had missed Jessica's call. What would she have said? *Guess what? I forgot all about Geoffrey today.*

Now she had to call Elaine. That was going to be hard, too. What was she going to tell her? *Going to a soccer game with Mason and Casey was more exciting than baby-sitting, so I forgot. . . .*

"Give me the phone," she said to Alex, holding out her hand.

"Jessica won't be home," he repeated.

"I *know*!" Abby said irritably.

"Grump," Alex said. He tossed it into her lap. "Don't be long. I'm waiting for Peter."

Abby stared at the phone. She picked it up and dialed the first five digits of Elaine's phone number. Then she pressed the OFF button.

She dialed again and hung up.

And again.

She couldn't do it.

She replaced the phone on its cradle and went to find her mother.

Her mother was in the kitchen, emptying the dishwasher. She frowned when she saw Abby.

"Elaine called," she said.

"I'm sorry!" Abby cried. "I forgot!!!"

"She had an important project to finish. She was counting on you."

"Sorry!" Abby said again.

Her mother continued. "She couldn't find another baby-sitter to replace you. Isabel offered to go over there."

Abby flushed red. Not only had she messed up, but her older sister had saved the day. How much worse could it get?

"I think Isabel should take over baby-sitting Geoffrey until Jessica gets back," her mother finished.

"*What???*" Abby cried. "That's not fair!!"

Her mother shook her head. "If you're not responsible enough to show up at your job, why should she keep you?"

Abby stared at her mother in dismay. This was a disaster.

"It was just once! Just one little mistake," Abby

pleaded. "And I'm really sorry. I'll never do it again."

"Sorry isn't enough. Elaine needs a reliable baby-sitter. If you go off to a soccer game with your friends, what's she supposed to do?"

"I get the point," Abby muttered.

She had known that everyone would be mad, but she never thought she'd lose the job. How could she ever tell Jessica?

Her mother put away the last clean dish.

"You owe Elaine an apology and Isabel a thank-you," she said. "I'm disappointed in you, Abby."

Abby went to her room and sat on the bed. For once, the bright purple walls failed to cheer her up.

She picked up her journal, then put it down.

The phone rang. She picked it up and pressed the ON button.

"Hello," she muttered into the receiver.

"Abby, it's Natalie! Where have you been?"

"Out," Abby said in a depressed voice. Natalie didn't seem to notice.

"I've been calling you all morning and getting a busy signal. Guess what?"

Abby sighed.

"We finally decided on a movie last night after school," Natalie announced. "It was a surprise win for *Merlin's Magic School*!"

"A fantasy?"

"Yep," Natalie said.

"How did you get everyone to vote for it?" Abby asked.

"A lot of kids wanted it." Natalie paused dramatically. "And Brianna made a speech in favor of it."

"Brianna??"

"Brianna's mother's aunt's third cousin's husband's sister-in-law has a cameo role in *Merlin's Magic School*."

"Oh, wow," Abby said.

"We're going to serve donuts and cider and call them Dragon Rings and Toad's Blood," Natalie continued. "Brianna suggested we all come in costume."

"Brianna will be a toad?" Abby asked hopefully.

"She's planning to dress as a sorceress."

"An evil one," Abby said. "And you'll be Merlin."

"Of course!" Natalie agreed.

"What about me?" Abby asked. "Who will I be?

One of the apprentices?"

"If you want. You don't *have* to come in costume," Natalie reassured her. "All you have to do is get the posters out."

"Oh, right, the posters," Abby mumbled. She didn't feel like thinking about them right now.

"We'll have huge crowds!" Natalie cried. "Once we get the word out, every kid under twelve will want to come. Be sure to put them all over town!"

"How long do I have?"

"Ten days. We have to have them up at least a week before movie night."

"Okay." Abby sighed deeply. "I have other things on my mind today."

"Like what?" Natalie asked.

"Stuff," Abby replied. She changed the subject. "Too bad Jessica's going to miss the movie."

"I think she's having fun in Oregon," Natalie said.

"Did you talk to her?" Abby cried eagerly. "How is she?"

"She's going to a dance party."

"A dance party? *Jessica?*"

"Yep," Natalie said.

"Did she say anything about me?"

"We only talked for five minutes," Natalie said. "I told her about the dogs. How was Geoffrey today?"

"He was . . . uh — "

"Do you need help with the posters?" Natalie interrupted.

"No, thanks. I'll start working on them this weekend. Geoffrey was — " Abby tried again and stopped. "I — "

She couldn't say another word. It was too painful.

"I've got to go," Natalie said. "Bethany and I are going out for ice cream. Want to come?"

"No money," Abby said. She had spent most of it this morning at the soccer game and she wouldn't be earning more in the future. Her parents wouldn't be handing her any cash, either. Not after today.

"Maybe another time," Natalie said.

"Maybe," Abby repeated.

Maybe another time she'd tell Natalie what had happened.

"Good-bye," she said glumly. She hung up the phone.

The walls of her room were just as purple. The calendars were just as numerous. Nothing had changed. Except now, on top of everything else, she had a poster to think about.

It would have to be a magnificent poster: exciting, dramatic, and irresistible. A poster that would prove she knew how to do *something* right. Maybe she'd use glitter pens and stickers on each one.

She didn't have any money to buy supplies, though.

Abby felt even worse than she had before Natalie called.

Chapter 9

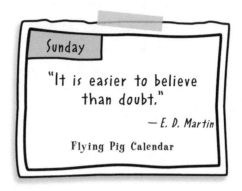

> **Sunday**
>
> "It is easier to believe than doubt."
>
> — E. D. Martin
>
> **Flying Pig Calendar**

For my best friend, it is easier to doubt than believe.

Jessica found out what happened and wrote me a long e-mail. She was very upset.

<u>Jessica doubts</u>

1. that Abby can hold down a job.

2. that Abby can remember she has a job.

3. that Abby is responsible and mature.

4. that Abby cares about her friends.

My best friend has lost trust in me!!!!!!!!

So has Elaine. She told Isabel that Jessica had given me an excellent recommendation. She was disappointed and angry when I didn't show up. I have lost my babysitting job, Jessica's trust, and Elaine's confidence.

(We pause for a moment of quiet despair.)

What to Do, Part One

1. Cry quietly in my room for ten minutes.
2. Get up, blow nose, and wipe eyes.
3. Look at face in mirror.
4. Decide to go out and get fresh air.
5. Try to avoid seeing anyone as I slip out of the house.
6. Walk along the streets, kicking at fallen leaves.
7. Feel miserable and alone.
8. Wish for someone

to wave a magic wand and change my life completely.

9. Not pay any attention to where I'm going or who's near me.

10. Bump into a large body who yelps in surprise.

Life, Limb, and Leaf
A true story by Abby Hayes

"Watch it!" Mason yelled.

"Sorry!" the distressed fifth-grader apologized. "I didn't see you."

"Did you have your eyes closed?" Casey asked. "No one can miss Mason."

"I'm unmissable," bragged the Mason Man.

"Did I hurt you?" she asked, feeling even worse than before. On top of everything else, she was crashing into innocent bystanders.

"Eeerp," Mason burped. "I've got too many layers on." He waved a puffy, down-filled sleeve in the air.

"We've been working all afternoon," Casey

explained, holding up a rake. "It's chilly to-day."

"I guess," Abby said. The wind blew her curly red hair into her face. She pushed it away with numb fingers.

"Wasn't the soccer game great yesterday?" Mason said.

Abby sighed tragically. "It's because of that soccer game that everyone's mad at me."

Casey raked some leaves into a pile. "What? For missing baby-sitting once?"

"Kathleen forgets things all the time!" Mason said. "Her homework, her gym clothes, her contact lenses, her brain."

"Neither of my sisters forgets anything, ever. They're so responsible that no one would even believe it if they messed up!" Abby cried. "And Jessica's the same way!"

"Gee, that's too bad," Mason said sympathetically.

"It won't happen again," Casey reassured her. "For the rest of your life, you'll never, ever forget a baby-sitting date. My mother says all you need is one big mistake to learn from."

Abby looked down at the ground. "I don't get a second chance," she said miserably. "Elaine fired me and hired my sister instead."

"That stinks!" Mason yelled.

"Yeah," Casey agreed.

"Jessica is furious, too. She thinks I'm irresponsible," Abby concluded. "How can I show her that I'm not?"

Casey leaned his rake against a tree. "Ask Geoffrey's mother to give you another try."

"_No_!" Abby cried. "Never!"

Mason belched loudly.

"Is that your suggestion for Abby?" Casey asked.

Mason brandished his rake in the air. "Why don't you rake leaves with us? We have more work than we can handle."

"That won't prove anything to Jessica," she said.

344

"You'll earn money," Casey pointed out. "And have fun with me and the Mason Man."

Abby sniffed and wiped her nose. She rubbed her two cold hands together and drew her scarf tighter around her neck.

She needed money. She _really_ needed fun.

"When do I start?" she asked.

What to Do, Part Two

1. Run home.

2. Change into warmer clothes. Put on down jacket and fleece hat. Find winter gloves.

3. Run into kitchen.

4. Announce to mother that I will be raking leaves with Casey and Mason all afternoon.

5. Agree to be home before dark.

6. Leave before anyone can say a word about yesterday.

Chapter 10

Friday morning

"Promise, large promise,
is the soul of an
advertisement."
—*Samuel Johnson*
Great Big Calendar of Soup Labels

Or the soul of a poster.

<u>What my poster will promise</u>
1. A movie full of adventure and magic
2. Delicious refreshments
3. Costumes and entertainment
4. Money donated to charity

Are these large enough promises? Will they make everyone want to come to the Silver Screen Savers movie night??

<u>What my poster will look like</u>

1. Bright fluorescent colors: green, pink, turquoise, and coral
2. Big lettering
3. Bold illustrations of stars and donuts (Dragon Rings). (I hope the Dragon Rings don't look like breakfast cereal!)
4. Glittery designs and rainbow stickers

Mom and I bought supplies for the poster on Wednesday. I earned enough money from raking leaves for plenty of pens and stickers! I designed the poster on the computer last night and printed a few out.

Maybe I'll get one of my friends to look at the poster before I distribute it. I want it to be <u>perfect</u>!!!

Tomorrow Dad will drive me around to put it up in stores, schools, and on bulletin boards all over the city. Then I'll call the local radio and television stations.

By the end of the weekend, the entire city will be lining up to buy tickets for the Silver Screen Savers movie night!!

"**H**ave you heard anything from Jessica?" Natalie asked Abby as they left Lancaster Elementary at the end of the day.

The two girls were on their way to Abby's house to look at the movie-night poster.

"Not lately," Abby said, adjusting the straps of her backpack. It wasn't exactly a lie. She hadn't heard from Jessica since last weekend.

"Jessica hasn't written or called me, either," Sarah chimed in, joining them as they crossed the playground.

"Is it us? Or is it her?" Abby asked. She had been worrying all week because Jessica hadn't responded to her note of apology.

"Dunno." Sarah shrugged.

"We should send an electronic greeting from the three of us," Natalie said. "Something funny."

"Great idea!" Sarah said. She pulled a red-patterned ski cap over her curly brown hair.

Abby didn't say anything.

"Have a good weekend, girls!" Ms. Yang, the principal, stood on the playground, watching the students leave.

"Thanks, Ms. Yang!" Natalie said.

The three girls strolled down the street.

"Why don't we send a greeting to Jessica right now?" Natalie suggested. "We'll use Abby's computer. Want to come with us, Sarah?"

"Yes!" Sarah said enthusiastically. She turned to Abby. "Okay?"

"Uh, sure, okay." Abby wished that Natalie had asked her first before inviting Sarah to *her* house.

Natalie skipped a few feet ahead, then faced the two girls. "Sarah, you can help us with the poster, too. Abby wants feedback. Right, Abby?"

"Right," Abby muttered. Did she have a choice? Natalie was making all the decisions.

Sarah rummaged in her pockets and pulled out a stick of gum. "Do you have snacks at your house?" she asked Abby.

"The usual boring stuff," Abby said. "Granola bars, graham crackers, cheese puffs."

"I love cheese puffs!" Sarah said, unwrapping the gum and putting it in her mouth.

The three girls turned down Abby's street.

Abby looked up as bright crimson leaves fluttered down from a maple tree. "More raking to do," she said.

"Was that you with Mason and Casey last week?" Sarah asked Abby.

Abby nodded.

She had spent most of her afternoons that week working. She, Casey, and Mason had each made twenty dollars. They had been treated to cookies, hot chocolate, and orange juice. They had gotten lots of exercise and met some friendly neighbors.

Once she saw Elaine and Geoffrey walking down the street together. Abby had hidden behind a tree until they passed.

Mason and Casey teased her about it for the rest of the afternoon.

Automatically, Abby glanced around to see if the boys were raking today. She wondered if they had any extra jobs and if they'd call her.

"You were raking leaves with *MasonandCasey*?" Natalie cried. She pronounced their names as if they were one word.

"Yep." Abby ran up the porch stairs and unlocked the front door of her house.

"But they're — they're — " For once Natalie was at a loss for words.

"Boys?" Abby finished.

"Disgusting boys," Natalie said. "Especially Mason."

"Casey is really nice," Abby protested. "And so is Mason. Once you get to know him. And his mom is so funny."

"Ugh," Natalie said.

Sarah made a face. "I can't stand Casey. He always makes stupid jokes."

Abby slammed the front door shut. The three girls dropped their backpacks in the hallway.

Natalie took off her jacket and walked into the living room. "Which computer are we using?"

"The downstairs one."

"Let's get a snack first," Sarah said.

"Is that all you think about?" Natalie asked.

"Yes!" Sarah retorted.

"The cheese puffs are in the kitchen cupboard," Abby said to Natalie. "Eat all you want."

Abby pointed them in the direction of the kitchen and went to find a poster for them to see.

A few minutes later, the three girls sat around the kitchen table. Abby had taped a fluorescent green poster on the wall above the table.

Natalie and Sarah studied it.

"So? What do you think?" Abby asked.

"You forgot to put the time on it," Natalie said.

"I did?" Abby cried. She jumped up and scrutinized the poster. "I *did*!"

Natalie took a handful of cheese puffs and put them in her mouth. Orange cheese dust covered her lips.

"Mfooellionto," she said.

"Don't talk with your mouth full!" Sarah said.

"I mean, that's easy to fix," Natalie said.

She pointed to the poster. "And don't forget to say that refreshments will be served by fifth-graders in costumes!"

"I won't — I mean — I *didn't* forget," Abby said.

"Make the donuts larger," Natalie continued. "They look like breakfast cereal."

"Breakfast cereal?" Abby repeated. "Why not rings or halos?"

Natalie didn't reply. "The title of the movie should be larger," she said. "Can you put it into fancy type? Like calligraphy?"

"I guess," Abby said.

Natalie grabbed another handful of cheese puffs.

"Save some for me!" Sarah cried. "Don't hog them all!"

"Pleckifooey," Natalie mumbled, spewing more orange cheese dust on her face. "There's plenty for everyone."

Abby nibbled on a pretzel and studied her poster. It didn't need *that* much work. Or did it?

"It's time to e-mail Jessica," Natalie suddenly announced.

"Yes!" Sarah cried. She scooped up the final handful of cheese puffs.

"You took the last ones!" Natalie protested.

"Who pigged out just now?" Sarah demanded, eating the cheese puffs one by one.

"Come on, everyone," Abby said. "Cheese puffs aren't the most important thing in the world."

She sounded stuffy and grown-up, like a parent or teacher. Why was she so out of tune with her friends?

"Yes, they *are*!" Sarah and Natalie chimed in unison.

The two girls began to laugh. Sarah offered Natalie the last few puffs.

"These cheese puffs are slimy!" Natalie shrieked.

Sarah shrugged and popped them into her mouth.

Natalie stood up. She dusted off her hands and threw the crumpled bag into the garbage.

"Time to send the card," she announced again.

Sarah jumped up.

Abby glanced at her poster one last time. When she made all the changes, would the poster be so exciting and beautiful that people would rush to see the movie?

Maybe it still needed extra glitter. Or magic wizard stickers. Or colored markers, or —

Natalie tapped Abby on the shoulder. "Let's go!"

The three girls went to the computer to send the electronic greeting to Jessica. They logged on to an e-card site.

Natalie took charge again.

"This one," she said. Natalie clicked on the image of a barking dog, then wrote "Wish you were here!" and signed all of their names.

"What about a rainbow?" Sarah suggested.

"No," Natalie said.

She never used to be like this, Abby thought. Was it because Jessica was gone?

Natalie pointed to another card that had planets

revolving in a starry sky. It said, "You're out of this world!"

"Perfect!" Sarah cried. "Don't you think so, Abby?"

"Uh, yeah," Abby said.

Everything had changed in only a few short weeks. Natalie was bossy, Sarah was hanging around too much, Jessica wasn't speaking to her. . . .

Abby didn't know who her friends were anymore — or whether she even had any.

Chapter 11

Saturday

"Be busy and you will be safe."

—Ovid

Daily Match Calendar

My parents must be <u>very</u> safe! Because they are busier than anyone I know!

My dad:
1. Has to finish rush project.
2. Has to shop and do errands.
3. Has to bring car in for repair.
4. Is going out of town tomorrow with Eva to watch tournament.

My mom:
1. Has to review case for Monday court appearance.

2. Has her turn to carpool for Alex's chess club.

3. Must do week's worth of laundry.

4. Will entertain friends tonight at our house.

The only time Dad can take me out to distribute the posters is between eleven and twelve today. I have to knock on his office door at ten to eleven. He's leaving the house at eleven.

The posters are printed out and decorated with glitter and stickers. There's a rainbow-colored stack of them on my desk. After I'm done plastering them all over town, I'm going to rake leaves again with Mason and Casey!

That'll be more fun than spending time after school with my girlfriends! At least the boys don't boss me around!

Isabel and Eva are also busy. Eva is at a practice (surprise!). Isabel is baby-sitting for Geoffrey this morning (boohoo).

Last night, Mom asked me if I had apologized to Elaine yet.

"Uh, no, not really," I mumbled.

Mom just looked at me.

I couldn't say another word.

My room is clean and my Saturday morning chores are done. It's 10:25 A.M. I will offer to help her with the laundry. She'll find out that I'm <u>not</u> irresponsible and forgetful!

"Take the clothes out of the dryer and fold and sort them," Olivia Hayes told Abby.

"Should I put them in the laundry basket?" Abby asked.

"Sure," her mother replied. "Then we'll take them upstairs." She sorted through the dirty clothing in the hamper, then looked at Abby.

"Thanks for helping, hon. It's not often that I have volunteers to do laundry. No one enjoys it."

"I do!" Abby said, folding a pair of Eva's Lycra shorts and putting them on a pile of clothing. "Except when I'm down here all alone."

Her mother glanced around the basement. "It's gloomy and damp, isn't it?" She smiled. "It's much more fun with someone to talk to." She began throwing dark clothes into the machine.

"Jessica's mom puts everything in at once," Abby commented. "Lights and darks together."

Olivia Hayes shook her head. "I'd never do that. But then there are six of us and only two of them. They probably don't have much laundry."

"Now she has even less," Abby said.

"Have you heard from Jessica?" Olivia Hayes asked. "Does she like her father's family?"

"Uh . . . she's been too busy to write," Abby said quickly.

"I hope she's writing to her mother."

"She's in Greece," Abby said. "Remember?"

Her mother sighed. "Lucky woman."

She turned the dial on the washing machine. "Do you want to put the soap in?" she asked Abby.

"Yes!" Abby picked up the bottle and filled the cap with liquid detergent. Then she poured it into the machine.

She shut the lid. "Can I start the washing machine?" she asked.

Her mother nodded. "Pull the dial out."

Water began rushing into the machine. Abby went back to the dryer to finish folding clothes. Now her mother would really think that she was responsible and mature.

Her mother pulled out the lint screen to clean it. "Abby, don't avoid apologizing to Elaine," she said.

"Why?" Abby burst out. "Isabel took my place!"

"It's important to face up to your actions. Taking responsibility will give you strength," her mother said.

"It will?" Abby said doubtfully. She hadn't gotten any strength from apologizing to Jessica. She hadn't even gotten any answer!

"Yes," her mother said. "You'll see what happens when you do talk to Elaine."

"I don't want to — " Abby began, and then stopped. She *did* want to be responsible. She wanted her mother to be proud of her. She didn't want her mother to look at her in that disappointed way.

"Okay," she said. "I'll talk to her."

Abby and her mother climbed up the stairs to the kitchen, their arms laden with piles of neatly folded clothes. In the basement, the washing machine was churning out its last load.

"Where do I put these clothes?" Abby asked.

"Bring Eva's and Isabel's up to their rooms," her mother said. "I'll take care of the rest." She put a stack of dish towels on the countertop. "Thanks, Abby! You've been a great help."

Abby smiled. Now her mother would know that she was someone who could be counted on.

"Your help couldn't have come at a better time," her mother continued. "Your father and I are so busy today!"

"Yes, you are," Abby agreed, then suddenly yelled, "*Busy?* Oh, no! What time is it?"

Her mother glanced at her watch. "It's eleven-twenty," she said.

"But we were only downstairs for twenty minutes!" Abby cried.

"No, it was almost an hour," her mother said.

Her arms still full of folded clothes, Abby rushed upstairs. "Dad! Dad!"

She banged on his office door. Shorts and socks fell to the floor.

"Dad????"

Abby dumped Isabel's clothes in a pile on her bed. She left Eva's on her desk. Then she ran back downstairs.

"Where's Dad? Mom, do you know where he is?"

"I think he's out," her mother said. "The car is gone."

"*No!!!*" Abby cried.

"Is something wrong?" her mother asked.

Abby shook her head. She wasn't going to tell her mother she had forgotten to do something important again.

"Can you drive me around later?" she asked. "I need to put up some posters for movie night."

"Not today," her mother said. "Not tomorrow, either. I won't be able to do it until Wednesday."

"That's too late," Abby said.

"Ask your father," her mother said. "He'll help you."

"Sure, Mom," Abby said.

She went back to her room and looked at the pile of posters on her desk. What was she going to do now?

Chapter 12

Saturday 12:01 P.M.

"There is an exception to every rule."

Yardstick Calendar

<u>The Rule</u>

Abby forgets!!!!

<u>The Exception</u>

Hasn't shown up yet.
I wish it would.
I need it. I need it <u>now</u>!!!

How could I forget something this impor-tant AGAIN??? (Also on a Saturday morning. Is there something dangerous about Saturday mornings?)

<u>Why I Forgot</u>

1. I am wasting away with a mysterious brain disease that causes me to forget only essential and urgent things.
2. Aliens are beaming forgetful rays into my mind.
3. It's the water.
4. I forget why I forgot.

(Will put self in <u>Hayes Book of World Records</u> for Worst Excuses for Worst Behavior.)

Help! Help! <u>Help!</u>

Am I <u>really</u> hopeless? Will I <u>always</u> forget everything important???
OR . . .
Am I caught in a web of mistakes?

<u>Abby's Domino Mistake Theory</u>
1st Mistake: I forget about Geoffrey.
2nd Mistake: So I try to impress my mother.

3rd Mistake: So I miss my appointment with my father.

4th Mistake: So the posters don't get out.

5th Mistake: Yet to come . . .

Conclusion

A single mistake will lead to many others.

What next???

How do I stop the mistakes from happening??? How do I stop being forgetful? How do I start getting the posters up???

My father is busy for the rest of the weekend.

My mother is busy for the rest of the weekend.

No one can drive me to stores and schools where I need to put them up.

Will anyone come to movie night if the posters aren't out?

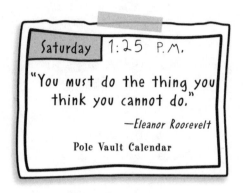

Saturday 1:25 P.M.

"You must do the thing you think you cannot do."

—Eleanor Roosevelt

Pole Vault Calendar

Drive a car????????

Other Solutions

1. Call a taxi (too expensive!).

2. Call someone else's parents and ask them (too embarrassing!).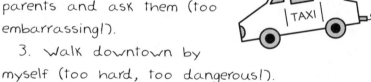

3. Walk downtown by myself (too hard, too dangerous!).

4. Ask my friends to help distribute the posters.

    a) Casey

    b) Mason (maybe)

    c) Natalie (can't admit what I've done)

    d) Bethany (obsessed with hamsters)

e) Jessica (in Oregon)
f) Brianna (forget it!)
g) Victoria (are you out of your mind?)
h) Sarah (naaaah...)
i) I'm running out of friends
   Casey is my only hope.

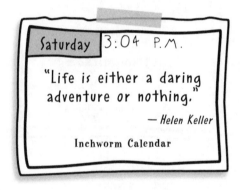

Saturday 3:04 P.M.

"Life is either a daring adventure or nothing."
— Helen Keller

Inchworm Calendar

Yes! I am about to embark on a daring adventure, thanks to Casey.

He suggested I turn the poster into a flyer.

I am printing out hundreds of copies right now.

Casey and I will distribute them to the entire neighborhood.

Hooray! Hooray! I <u>will</u> let people know about the Silver Screen Savers movie night. The school will be packed! We will raise lots of money for the relief fund. Our evening will be a success!

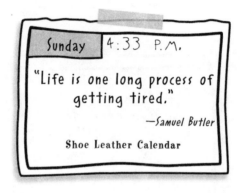

Sunday 4:33 P.M.

"Life is one long process of getting tired."

—Samuel Butler

Shoe Leather Calendar

Flyers distributed: 467
Posters posted: 8
Pairs of shoes worn out: 2
Aching toes: 20 (mine and Casey's)
Grateful friends: 1 (me)

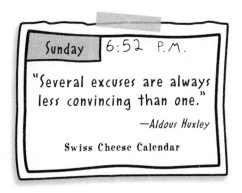

> Sunday 6:52 P.M.
>
> "Several excuses are always less convincing than one."
>
> —Aldous Huxley
>
> **Swiss Cheese Calendar**

Are ten excuses more convincing than two?

Or are two excuses more convincing than ten?

Is one excuse less convincing than <u>none</u>?

Are <u>all</u> excuses not convincing?

<u>No Excuse! A Phone Conversation</u>

The phone rings. Abby picks it up. It's Natalie.

Natalie: Hi, Abby!

Abby: Hi!

Natalie: Bethany and I were downtown today at the pet store. I got a new hamster cage for Madame Curie.

Abby: What color?

Natalie: Blue. (pauses for a moment) Bethany and I looked for posters, but we didn't see any.

Abby: Casey and I went door-to-door yesterday and today. We distributed almost five hundred flyers to the entire neighborhood.

Natalie: I still think we need the posters. What about the people who don't live in our neighborhood?

Abby (looks down at her sore feet): Oh, yeah. Right.

Natalie: Are you going to get them up soon?

Abby: I don't know. My parents are really busy.

Natalie: Bethany and I could have done a lot of them today. You should have asked us!

Abby is too embarrassed to reply. Natalie is right.

Natalie: Do you want us to take some?

Abby: No, no, it's okay. Don't worry — they'll be out by tomorrow.

Tuesday 5:21 P.M.

"Promises, promises . . ."

Santa's Wish List Calendar

Promises I Made

1. That two dozen posters (at least!) would be tacked to bulletin boards and community notice boards by tonight.

2. That every supermarket in town would have a poster advertising the Silver Screen Savers movie night.

3. That I would call the local radio and television stations and ask them to broadcast the news about our fund-raiser!

Promises I Kept

1. I called the radio and television stations. Both said I called too late. Even if I had called last weekend, it would have

been too late. They need ten days' advance notice!

2. I put up a poster at our local supermarket.

3. Isabel put up a poster at the library; Eva took one for the athletic center at the college.

Wednesday 8:47 P.M.

"Better late than never."

Procrastinator's Daily Calendar

The posters are FINALLY! up all over town. Dad was FINALLY! able to drive me around after school. We FINALLY! put them up in supermarkets, schools, drugstores, and gymnasiums.

The Silver Screen Savers movie night is

only two days away. That might not be enough time for people to see the posters.

I might have put them up too late. Late is sometimes NOT better than never.

Late is sometimes equal to never.

P.S. Don't let Natalie know. She thinks the posters went up on Monday.

Chapter 13

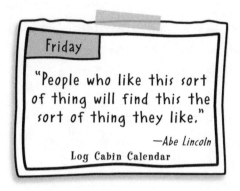

Friday

"People who like this sort of thing will find this the sort of thing they like."

—*Abe Lincoln*

Log Cabin Calendar

Our Silver Screen Savers movie night <u>will</u> <u>be</u> "the sort of thing people like"!

The Dough Re Mi Bakery has donated Dragon Rings (donuts) and Toad's Blood (cider).

We're also selling Wizard Bricks (brownies), Gobbles (popcorn), and Merlin's Brew (hot chocolate).

We will show cartoons, followed by the feature film.

Ms. Kantor's class will come dressed as characters from <u>Merlin's Magic School</u>.

I am an enchanted pen. I'm wearing a long purple robe with gold swirls, and my headpiece is a pen nib made of aluminum foil and duct tape.

Everything will be perfect. Our class has spent weeks preparing for this event.

Or almost perfect . . .

What if only two or three people show up?

What if no one eats the donuts, drinks the cider, or watches the movie?

What if we don't make any money to donate to the relief fund?

It will all be MY fault!!!!

As the van turned into the Lancaster Elementary school parking lot, Abby adjusted the silver mask over her eyes.

She wished that she could turn herself into a real

enchanted pen and write herself into another story.

Her father pulled into a parking spot and turned off the ignition. "You look very nice, honey," he said to Abby.

"Yeah," Abby mumbled. "Thanks."

"Do pens wear sneakers?" her father teased, pointing to the ones peeking out from underneath Abby's robe. "Did they have sneakers in Merlin's time?"

"Merlin used duct tape in his spells," Abby said.

"I forgot about that," her father said.

Abby pulled the robe up around her ankles and stepped out of the car. She glanced anxiously around the parking lot.

The lot was almost empty. What if not even two or three people showed up? What if *no one* showed up?

Slowly she walked toward the school.

"Abby!" Natalie called. She was wearing magician's robes and a tall, pointed hat. She had a wand in one hand and a book of magic spells in the other.

"You look great!" Abby cried.

"You, too," Natalie said. "What are you?"

"An enchanted pen," Abby said.

"You have the 'write' costume, Hayes," Casey said, coming up to them.

"Very punny, Hoffman," Abby retorted, forgetting her worries for a moment.

"Urp." A familiar-sounding burp echoed in the playground.

Abby turned around. Her mouth dropped open. "Is that . . . *Mason?*"

"Urp," he responded.

"Omigosh!" Natalie cried.

For once, even Casey was speechless.

Mason was wearing a black tuxedo with a pink shirt and a bow tie. His hair was slicked back from his face, and his shoes were shining.

"Urp," he said again.

"Could you repeat that, please?" Casey said. He held up his hand. "Just kidding. Don't say another word — or burp."

"You look like a butler," Natalie said.

"I'm an usher!" Mason muttered. "I'm going to take tickets and show the crowds into the gym."

"Crowds?" Abby repeated anxiously. "There aren't any."

"Just wait," Mason said, flinging out his arms. "We'll have to turn them away! We'll have to schedule another showing! We'll —"

"Mason!" Ms. Kantor cried. "We're waiting for

you." Her eyes widened. "Wow," she said. "Wowee."

"Cute!" Bethany squealed. She was dressed in her Halloween hamster costume.

Mason blushed.

"Come in, everyone!" Ms. Kantor said. "We still have plenty to do before the movie starts."

The fifth-graders hurried into the school.

Ms. Kantor gave out orders. "Abby, go in the gym and set up chairs. Natalie, check the refreshment table, and make sure the coffeemaker is plugged in. Bethany, find some tape to put up these signs."

"I'll help," Casey offered.

"Great!" Ms. Kantor said. "Why don't you go to the cafeteria and carry in the jugs of cider?"

Abby's father reached into his pocket. "I'd like to buy a ticket," he said.

"You're one of our first customers," Ms. Kantor said. "Mason is all set to take your money."

"Step right this way, sir," Mason said smoothly.

In the gym, a crew of kids in costumes was unfolding metal chairs and setting them in rows.

A scattering of people sat near the front. Abby counted them. There were twelve adults and kids.

"Why are there so few people?" Natalie demanded.

Abby jumped. She hadn't realized that Natalie was right behind her.

"Uh, well," Abby began.

Natalie didn't wait for an answer. She hurried away.

Abby took a deep breath and went to get a couple of chairs. She set them at the end of a row. Then she got some more.

Ms. Kantor came into the gym and surveyed the rows of chairs.

"Good job, chair crew!" She glanced at the clock, then at the people trickling into the gym.

She turned on the microphone.

"Good evening," Ms. Kantor greeted the audience. "Popcorn, brownies, and cider are for sale in the cafeteria. The movie will begin a little later than scheduled to give more people a chance to arrive. All profits will be donated to a disaster relief fund."

Mason was standing in front of the ticket table, talking to Bethany and Natalie.

"How many people have come in?" Natalie asked.

"Seventeen?" Mason said. "Maybe eighteen?"

Ms. Kantor hurried toward them. She checked her watch, then glanced at the front doors. The lobby was empty.

"Why isn't anyone here?" she asked. "I don't understand it."

Abby thought of the relief fund. Ms. Kantor's class wouldn't have any money to send to it now. Maybe enough for a couple of boxes of cereal, if they were lucky.

It should have been more.

"I got the posters out too late!" Abby cried. "No one saw them!"

Natalie frowned. Bethany and Mason looked surprised. Ms. Kantor cleared her throat.

"Abby, I wish you had spoken to me sooner," Ms. Kantor began.

"Sorry," Abby said miserably. "I'm really sorry."

The doors flew open. Brianna and Victoria entered the school.

Brianna was dressed as an enchantress in brilliant fire-red satin. She wore red high heels and red lipstick to match. She had a red sparkly crown in her long dark hair and a diamond necklace.

Her new best friend, Victoria, was dressed in a

blue lace T-shirt with a blue leather skirt and chunky shoes.

"You, like, look like a fire engine," she said to her best friend, loud enough for the rest of the class to hear.

"I'm in costume," Brianna announced haughtily.

"You're also late," Ms. Kantor said. "I asked everyone to be here before seven."

"Did you hear the radio announcement?" Brianna asked, putting her hand on her hip. "It said — "

"There wasn't any radio announcement," Abby mumbled. Her face was hot. "I called them too late!"

Brianna cut her off. "You don't have connections. My third cousin's aunt's brother-in-law *owns* the radio station. They've been announcing the Silver Screen Savers movie night every hour for the last three days. Don't you listen to WLXPOP, Tiffany Crystal's favorite station?"

"No," Abby said.

Brianna flipped her long dark hair over her shoulder. "Thanks to me, we'll have a crowd tonight."

"A *crowd*?" Natalie asked, gesturing at the empty lobby.

"Like, where is it?" Victoria said meanly. "I don't see any, like, sixth-grade boys, you know."

"The whole world listens to WLXPOP," Brianna said with a small shrug. "They'll be here. The people will come."

"For once, I hope she's right," Abby whispered to Casey, who had just joined them. "If she is, I'll be the first to yell, 'Yay, Brianna!' "

Ms. Kantor looked at her watch again. "There are no crowds. The movie was supposed to start ten minutes ago, and no one is here."

"The movie is supposed to start at seven-thirty," Brianna said smugly. "The radio announced the wrong time."

"It did??" Ms. Kantor cried.

"The posters and flyers announced seven P.M.," Abby said.

"No one reads those things!" Brianna dismissed her with a wave of the hand.

"Brianna," Ms. Kantor said, frowning. "Why didn't you tell us sooner?"

"Yeah!" Mason echoed. "How were we supposed to know?"

"Like, what's your problem, Tuxedo Man?" Victoria was suddenly on Brianna's side again. "Don't you listen to WLXPOP?"

"No!" Mason retorted.

"I don't listen to it, either," Natalie said.

"Me, neither," Bethany chirped.

"Or me!" Abby said.

"Where do they, like, come from?" Victoria asked her best friend.

Brianna adjusted her crown. "WLXPOP is the best station in town. The crowd will be here."

Ms. Kantor shook her head. "If the crowd doesn't show up *very soon*, I'm starting the movie."

"You'll see," Brianna promised.

The fifth-graders looked at each other. Mason burped. Natalie whispered to Bethany. Casey hummed a tune.

Brianna smiled at her reflection in the glass of the front doors. "Look!" she said, pointing triumphantly.

A group of people was approaching the front door.

Chapter 14

> **Friday**
>
> "A hard beginning makes a good ending."
>
> Days of Winter Calendar

Lots of people are here to see <u>Merlin's Magic School</u>! Mason can't sell tickets fast enough. Casey, Natalie, and Bethany are helping him. Almost every seat is filled!!!

Our hard beginning <u>didn't</u> make this good ending! Brianna made it.

Thanks to her, we will meet our expenses and have a large donation for the relief fund.

Thanks to her, our movie night is a success!

Thanks to her, I'm off the hook.

Sometimes Brianna really _is_ the best!

In recognition of her service to Ms. Kantor's fifth-grade class and to me, <u>The Hayes Book of World Records</u> will award Brianna a free one-day brag pass. She is entitled to unlimited bragging for twenty-four hours. No one will be allowed to complain!

Okay, I <u>promised</u> I'd do it:

Yay, Brianna. Yay, Brianna! <u>YAY, BRIANNA!</u>

P.S. I have only one problem left. Who am I going to sit with?

Natalie: Tells me what to do all the time now. Do I want to be lectured on my mistakes?

Sarah: Just don't like her very much.

Bethany: Sitting with Natalie and Sarah.

Casey: I'd like to sit with him, but if I do, my friends will tease me, and Brianna and Victoria will call us lovebirds.

Mason: *No, I don't think I want to sit with the Big Burper.*

Jessica: *In Oregon and mad at me.*

I guess I'll sit by myself.

Who cares??? Our movie night is a success!!!! Hooray!!!!

Abby stood at the bathroom sink, washing her hands. They were sticky from the jelly donuts she had eaten.

The movie was over. Now everyone was in the cafeteria feasting on Toad's Blood, Merlin's Brew, Gobbles, and Dragon Rings.

Abby dried her hands and checked her costume in the mirror. Her silver-foil pen nib was off to the side of her head. She adjusted it and brushed donut crumbs from the front of her robe.

For what seemed like the thousandth time that evening, she breathed a sigh of relief.

"This thing is *so* hot!" Bethany cried, coming into the bathroom. She pulled off her costume's hamster head. "You're smiling, Abby."

"Our Silver Screen Savers movie night was a success!" Abby explained.

Bethany splashed water on her flushed face. "Of course it was. Why wouldn't it be?"

"*Me*," Abby said. "Didn't you hear? I got the posters up late!" She sighed. "I wish no one knew. Especially Natalie."

"Why?" Bethany asked. "I thought you were best friends."

Abby shrugged.

"It's just a mistake," Bethany said.

"I've made a *lot* of them," Abby said. "Especially since Jessica left. I haven't been myself in a while."

"Who's that?" Bethany teased.

She gave Abby a quick hug. "Natalie will understand."

"Maybe," Abby said. She hoped Bethany was right. "Too bad Elaine won't," she added.

"Elaine?" Bethany wiped her face with a paper towel.

"Geoffrey's mother." Abby lowered her voice. "I got fired from my baby-sitting job. All I did was forget one time."

"That's too bad," Bethany said sympathetically.

"I wish she had given me another chance,"

Abby said. "Or maybe not. Geoffrey is a handful."

Bethany giggled. "I heard about the maple syrup in Jessica's hair."

"He's a terror with chocolate pudding, too."

Bethany lowered the hamster head back onto her head. "How does Jessica do it?"

"She had special Geoffrey-taming tricks." Abby sighed. "And she never forgets anything."

Bethany waved to Abby. "See you at the refreshment stand?"

Abby bent down to tie her sneaker. A toilet flushed, and one of the stall doors swung open.

A woman came out and glanced at Abby. She went to the sink and turned on the water.

Abby stood up. She brushed off her robe one last time. Her eyes met the eyes of the woman in the mirror. It was Elaine.

"Uh . . ." she stammered. "Uh . . ."

Elaine's lips tightened. She turned off the water, dried her hands with a paper towel, and hurried away without a word.

Her face burning, Abby stumbled out of the bathroom.

Had Elaine heard *every* word she said?

In the cafeteria, a group of fifth-graders gathered to watch Mason pop donuts in his mouth, one after another.

"Six, seven, eight," the kids chanted.

"How many donuts can Mason eat?" Natalie cried.

"Like, millions," Victoria said.

"Urp," Mason said.

"Join us!" Casey called.

Abby gazed miserably around her. The last thing she wanted was to watch a donut-eating contest. Why hadn't she talked about hamsters, Bethany's favorite subject?

Her father tapped her on the shoulder. "It's time to leave," he said.

"Good," Abby said.

"The movie was great!" Alex cried. He had come with his friend Peter. "Did you like it, Abby?"

"Sure." She pulled her coat over her costume and followed her father, her brother, and his friend out to the parking lot.

Paul Hayes unlocked the van. "Everyone in!" he ordered.

Alex and Peter tumbled into the backseat.

Her father put his hand on Abby's shoulder. "You should be proud of yourself, honey," he said. "It was a terrific fund-raiser!"

"Thanks," Abby mumbled.

Her father brushed a light dusting of snow from the windshield.

Abby glanced at her classmates returning to their cars. Brianna and Victoria were arguing loudly as Brianna's mother honked the horn to get their attention.

"Just a minute, Dad," Abby said suddenly. "I'll be right back."

She dashed across the lot and came to a halt, breathless, in front of Elaine and Geoffrey.

Chapter 15

Saturday

"Nothing is ever said that has not been said before."

—Terence

Carbon Copy Calendar

<u>What I said to Elaine</u>

1. "Um, uh . . ."
2. "Uh, I, uh . . ."
3. "I, uh, well . . ."
4. "Oh, uh, um . . ."

Has anyone said this before? I hope so. I'd hate to be the first person who stuttered and stammered this way.

<u>What I said to Elaine next</u>

1. "I, uh, um . . . I'm . . ."
2. "I'm, uh, ssss – "

3. "What I, um . . . I mean . . .
uh . . ."

4. "Well . . . oh . . . uh . . . uh . . ."

Has someone said that, too?

Elaine didn't say anything. She just
waited. If she had said something, it might
have been easier. It also might have been
harder.

Finally I took a breath. "I – I'm sorry I
forgot about baby-sitting Geoffrey."

Elaine nodded.

"Um . . . I hope I never do it again."

"I hope not," Elaine said. She didn't
look too friendly. "If it hadn't been for
your sister, I would have lost a morning's
work."

"Sorry!" I said.

Geoffrey made a face at me.

"Jessica never forgot," Elaine continued.
"I thought you'd be reliable."

"It was just once," I muttered miserably.

"Once too many," Elaine said.

"Sorry," I said again.

Elaine didn't reply.

"Well, see you around," I said.

I ran back to the car.

My father was sitting behind the wheel. As I slid into the front seat, he patted my arm.

"That took courage," he said.

"Really?"

"Yes!" my father said.

"It didn't go very well," I mumbled.

"You apologized, didn't you?" he asked.

"Yes, but — "

"She was still angry?"

I nodded.

"Then it took even more courage to apologize," my father said.

"Well . . ."

"I'm proud of you." My father turned the key in the ignition and backed slowly out of the parking space.

"Really?" I didn't believe him.

"You faced up to a mistake. You didn't run away from what you had done."

I took a deep breath. "I was trying to do something right for a change."

My father nodded. "You won't ever forget a baby-sitting date again," he promised.

"No!" I cried. "I'll tie a hundred pieces of string around my fingers, write the times on every calendar in my room, put signs on the bathroom mirror and the front and back doors . . ."

Alex leaned forward. "I'll put a reminder in the computer for you, Abby," he offered.

"Okay," I said. "It's a deal."

Bethany just called. We made $418.50 for the relief fund!

Hooray! Hooray! Hooray!

Ms. Kantor said to Natalie and Bethany and Mason that she was very proud of the entire class. She called the newspaper to tell them what we had done. A photographer will come to our class on Monday. We are going to have our pictures in the paper.

Speaking of relief . . .
I am more relieved than anyone in the

fifth grade!!! My bad luck has finally broken!!

PHEW!!!! Stretch arms and touch toes.
Hop around purple room. Pick up phone and
call Jessica in Oregon. Has my bad luck
broken there, too?
   She hasn't written me in more than a week.
I <u>HAVE</u> to know if we're still friends.

<u>Notes after a Phone Conversation</u>

1. What the girl who answered the phone
called her: "Jessy."

2. Who Jessica thought I was: Someone
named Madison.

3. When Jessica got my e-mail: More
than a week ago.

4. Why she didn't write back: She forgot.
(<u>Ha!</u> So I'm <u>NOT</u> the only one!!!)

5. What she talked about: Dances, boys,
lip gloss, new clothes.

6. What she didn't talk
about: Our friends, science,
drawing, Ms. Kantor's class,
movie night.

7. What I said: Almost nothing.
8. How the conversation ended: Danielle called for Jessy to help her pick the right necklace for the dance tonight.

The Good News
Jessica isn't mad at me anymore.

The Bad News
Who is <u>Jessy</u>?

The Old News
I miss Jessica.

The New News
<u>Jessy</u> doesn't miss me.

The Worst News
<u>Jessy</u> and I don't have much in common. We might not even like each other anymore. This is even more horrible than Jessica being mad at me!

<u>What to Do</u>

1. Cry.
2. Write in journal.
3. Look at face in mirror.
4. Comb hair. Wipe eyes. Stick out tongue.
5. Start to cry again.

INTERRUPTION! Alex just knocked on the door. Casey is here to see me.

<u>What to Do, Part Two</u>

1. Wipe eyes again. Blow nose. Make face at self in mirror.
2. Put on sunglasses to hide red eyes.
3. Go downstairs. Say hi to Casey.
4. Say yes when Casey asks if I want to ride my bike with him this afternoon.

Go outside. See bright sunshine. Take deep breath. Climb on bike. Ride to park and race Casey around the fountain. Win. Laugh. Race again.

Read more books about me!

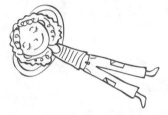

SPEND YOUR DAY THE ABBY WAY!

The Amazing Days of Abby Hayes® by Anne Mazer

In a family of superstars, it's hard to stand out. But Abby is about to surprise her friends, her family, and most of all, herself!

Hang out with Abby at
www.scholastic.com/abbyhayes

Have you read them all?

❑	0-439-14977-0	#1 Every Cloud Has a Silver Lining	$4.99
❑	0-439-17876-2	#2 The Declaration of Independence	$4.99
❑	0-439-17877-0	#3 Reach for the Stars	$4.99
❑	0-439-17878-9	#4 Have Wheels, Will Travel	$4.99
❑	0-439-17881-9	#5 Look Before You Leap	$4.99
❑	0-439-17882-7	#6 The Pen Is Mightier Than the Sword	$4.99
❑	0-439-35366-1	#7 Two Heads Are Better Than One	$4.99
❑	0-439-35367-X	#8 The More, the Merrier	$4.99
❑	0-439-35368-8	#9 Out of Sight, Out of Mind	$4.99
❑	0-439-35369-6	#10 Everything New Under the Sun	$4.99
❑	0-439-48273-9	#11 Too Close for Comfort	$4.99
❑	0-439-48280-1	#12 Good Things Come in Small Packages	$4.99
❑	0-439-48281-X	#13 Some Things Never Change	$4.99
❑	0-439-48282-8	Super Special #1 The Best Is Yet to Come	$5.99
❑	0-439-63775-9	Super Special #2 Knowledge Is Power	$5.99
❑	0-439-68063-8	#14 It's Music to My Ears	$4.99
❑	0-439-68066-2	#15 Now You See It, Now You Don't	$4.99
❑	0-439-68067-0	#16 That's the Way the Cookie Crumbles	$4.99

■SCHOLASTIC

ABB1105

Who said being a princess was easy?

Cinderella, Sleeping Beauty, Snow White, and Rapunzel share more than a locker at the Princess School. Despite dealing with witches, evil stepmothers, and Frog Identification class, these damsels aren't too distressed to have a ball.

www.scholastic.com/princessschool

The Princess School

DEAR DUMB DIARY

In Jamie Kelly's hilarious, candid (and sometimes not-so-nice) diaries, she promises everything she writes is true...or at least as true as it needs to be!

www.scholastic.com/deardumbdiary

Available wherever you buy books.

www.scholastic.com

SCHOLASTIC

FILLGIRL3

One false move could blow their cover.

by Christine Harris

TOP SECRET

Jesse Sharpe is an orphan, a genius, and a secret agent. Working for a mysterious organization, she trails suspects, cracks codes, and kicks butt in a world where she can trust no one but herself.

UNDERCOVER GIRL

by Peter Lerangis

SPY X

Twins Evie and Andrew must navigate a maze of intrigue and espionage as they race to uncover the truth about their mother's disappearance.

CLASSIFIED

www.scholastic.com

Available wherever you buy books.

SCHOLASTIC

FILLGIRL1

Special Bonds with Special Friends

Paws, hoofs, or fins — Mandy is there to lend a helping hand as she rescues animals in need.

By Ben M. Baglio

Nestled in the foothills of Virginia, there's a place where horses come when they are hurt. Amy, Ty, and everyone at Heartland work together to heal the horses—and form lasting bonds that will touch your heart forever.

Healing horses, healing hearts...

By Lauren Brooke

Chestnut Hill

By Lauren Brooke

From the author of the Heartland books comes a smart, sassy series set at an exclusive all-girls boarding school in Virginia, where horses—and winning—mean everything.